MATTHEW DANTE

Bikers of Mayhem
Book 4

UNTAMED AGGRESSION

BIKERS OF MAYHEM
BOOK 4

MATTHEW DANTE

Untamed Aggression (Bikers of Mayhem - Book 4)

Cover by **The Ravens Touch** @the.ravens.touch
Edited by Steph White (Kat's Literary Services)

Warning: This book contains scenes of violence, murder, kidnapping, and attempted sexual assault.

ISBN eBook: 978-1-997751-07-6

Paperback: 978-1-997751-06-9

CONTENTS

PROLOGUE

MARCUS

Using his butt, Marcus pushed open the back door and let himself into the kitchen.

"Oh good. You're back," Marcus heard his stepmother say as he walked through the door.

His back was to her, so he couldn't see where she was. He let out a huff as he dropped the bags of groceries onto the kitchen counter.

"What did you bring?" his stepmom asked, shoving Marcus out of the way so she could bend over and begin rummaging through the bags.

"Just the usual—bread, eggs, milk, and meat for dinner," Marcus answered, annoyed that his stepmother was acting like a vulture.

It was always the same with his parents; they never did anything to help out around the house, but they were always the first to pick the refrigerator clean when Marcus did the grocery shopping—which was basically every week.

"Oh good, you're back," Marcus's father repeated as he walked into the kitchen carrying his ragged riding knapsack. The damn thing was older than time itself.

Marcus glanced down at the kitchen table and noticed the small overnight bag his stepmom used for her personal items: makeup, condoms, and travel-sized tequila. All the essentials a biker chick needed when hitting the road with her man.

"Wh-what are you doing?" Marcus asked as his father shoved his wallet into the back of his jeans.

"What does it look like?" his father asked, throwing him a ridiculous face as he picked up a bottle of gin and shoved it into his wife's bag. "Packing a fuckin' bag is what we're doin'."

"Your dad and I are going to take a ride out west. Hit a few bars, take in some sites. We'll probably crash at one of those motels by the side of the road. We should be back by mid-next week."

Marcus looked at them both as they continued to pack like nothing was wrong.

"But... you can't!" Marcus shouted.

Both his parents stopped what they were doing and looked over at him.

"And why is that?" Marcus's father asked, straightening up and giving him a pissed-off look. If there was one thing you didn't do, it was question the big guy or raise your voice to him.

"You promised to take Ace to the water park today. He's been looking forward to it all week. I even bought him those gummy wrap things that he likes," Marcus said, pulling out the box of candy snacks from the bag he was holding.

Marcus's stepmother scrunched her face. "Oh, Ace doesn't give a crap about some stupid water park. He probably won't even remember we said we were going to go when he wakes up." She returned to her packing. "Don't worry, we'll take him another time."

That was the same thing she had been saying for the past two months. Summer was quickly coming to an end. If they didn't go soon, his little brother wouldn't get to go until next year.

"No. He won't forget. You promised him that you would take him, so you're going to do it," Marcus barked back.

His father was suddenly in his face.

"Don't talk to your mother like that, you hear?"

Marcus glared at the piece of shit that squirted him from his balls twenty-three years ago. While Marcus was all grown and didn't need shit from his parents, Ace was only ten. He still believed the things his parents said.

"Oh, and make sure you clean up this place before we get back. It's starting to develop a funky smell around the living room," his father ordered.

Marcus glared at his father.

One day, the lazy-ass would suffer a little accident. Perhaps his brakes would fail, or he would take a corner too fast, but one day, Marcus's father and Ace's mother would not make it back from their road trips.

Shoving a few items into the fridge, Marcus watched as his stepmother helped herself to a few of the things he had just purchased and shoved them into her bag.

Lazy fuckers.

Once the roar of his father's motorcycle had disappeared down the block, Marcus picked up his cell phone and scrolled through his contact list.

"Hey, Michelle, sorry, but I can't make our date today. Yeah, I know it's last minute, but my parents flaked, and I've got to take my little bro out to the water park today."

Marcus listened as Michelle barked back at him, complaining that this was bullshit, and she was tired of always being pushed aside.

"Look, we can go tomorrow. I just can't abandon my brother today. He's been looking forward to this outing all week."

Marcus felt bad that he was canceling his date at the last minute, but his little brother came first. While their parents might not give a shit about them, Marcus was sure as hell going to show his little brother that he cared, even if he was only Ace's stepbrother.

The little dude deserved the world. Marcus's love life could wait.

Growing tired of the woman yelling at him over the phone, Marcus decided to bark back.

"Look, I'm sorry if you can't understand what family means. But to me, family comes first. So go enjoy your time in Arizona, and don't ever call me again, bitch."

The line went dead.

Fucking bitch.

He and Michelle had only recently started dating. They had hooked up at a friend's bonfire party—well, actually, it had been Michelle riding his dick, while her roommate rode his face. Marcus had decided to date Michelle because she was the one with the bigger tits. She was the one who had suggested they go away for a few days, just the two of them. Marcus got the sense that she was just trying to get him away from his brother and the guys.

Some women just craved all the attention.

"Marcus? Why are you yelling?" a sleepy voice asked from behind him.

Marcus turned around just as a little dude wearing race-car pajamas entered the kitchen, rubbing his eyes.

It was only after he lowered his hands that realization set in.

"Yay! Water park! Today is the day!"

Ace began jumping up and down, pumping his fists in the air with so much excitement.

It was because of this reaction that Marcus knew he

couldn't let his little brother down. Even if their parents were pieces of shit, he was not going to be.

"Yes. Today, we are going to the water park!" Marcus cheered, reaching down and scooping up his little brother. "Do you know what ride you want to try first?"

"The big one that goes down and then like this." Ace used his hand to mimic the path of a water slide.

Marcus had never been to the park, but he guessed they all looked alike.

He placed his brother down on the floor and tousled his hair.

"Okay, go put on your swimsuit, and I'll finish packing our lunches."

Ace ran off with a squeal, apparently not even noticing that his parents were nowhere to be found.

It was nothing new for them. It was a rare occasion when their parents were ever around.

1

GAVIN

Staring at his reflection in the mirror, Gavin took a deep breath, hoping to calm his nerves. He knew he was being dramatic. People went on first dates all the time, but this one, he had a feeling about.

The man sounded too good to be true. He was a plastic surgeon, had a large family, was an Aries, and was just two years out of a long-term relationship, so you know he no longer holds a torch for his ex.

Everything had to go perfectly.

This guy might be *the one*.

They were all *the one* whenever he went out on a first date.

That was the problem with hopeless romantics: They never have realistic expectations. Everything has to be bigger, more over-the-top, and beyond belief.

Hopeless romantics didn't just settle for the mundane. They wanted excitement and surprise! Something that would make all others envious.

Reaching into his pocket, Gavin pulled out his phone and switched the camera view so he was able to record his reflection in the fancy restaurant lobby mirror.

This, here, was for his fans.

"Hey, everyone, Gavin here. Tonight, I wanted to give you all a one-of-a-kind exclusive into my first date with Mr. Surgeon. You'll be the first to hear how my hot and steamy date went... fingers crossed."

Gavin held up his crossed fingers and said a silent prayer up to the heavens. He really needed this date to go well. He was getting pretty lonely and was so fucking horny.

It had been ages since he dated anyone, and he was getting tired of the random hookups on sex apps. They all felt the same: an awkward hello, followed by fifteen minutes of desperate humping, then a hurried goodbye with no follow-up plans to meet up again.

He just wanted someone nice to talk to and some good, old, reliable dick.

Was that too much to ask for?

"Tonight, we will be dining at *Restaurante Piccolo* right here in beautiful Colorado. I'm just about to head in and meet my date for the first time in person! He sounds amazing in his profile, so let's hope that this one isn't a dud. Wish me luck!"

With that, Gavin ended the recording and posted it on his social media. That should get his followers talking.

Gavin took a breath and slid his phone back into his pocket. He took one last look at himself in the mirror and grimaced when he saw his hair. He pushed down that stubborn piece of hair that kept plaguing him. He looked like a goddamn cockatoo.

His hair sprang back up, but this time it was not as noticeable.

"Well, here goes nothing." Gavin exhaled at his reflection. He turned and smiled at the hostess waiting behind her podium.

"Hi there, I'm meeting someone. The reservation is under Ashford. Robert Ashford."

"Oh, your party is already here," the woman graciously noted.

Of course he was. Gavin was running late, once again. Would he ever be on time for anything in his life?

Gavin gave the woman a weary smile as she offered to escort him to the table.

Soft brown eyes greeted Gavin when he arrived at the table, followed by a warm and inviting smile.

The man stood, happy to see him.

"Gavin? It's a pleasure to meet you," the man said, offering Gavin his hand and giving it a firm handshake when he accepted it.

"Wow, good-looking and has manners," Gavin noted, releasing the man's hand and taking a seat across from him. “I’m so sorry I’m late. Once again, couldn’t find anything good enough to wear.”

“That’s not true. You look amazing in what you’re wearing,” the man offered, smiling at him while making Gavin feel like the luckiest guy in the world.

Perhaps this was *the one*, after all.

“You really are a sweetheart,” Gavin admitted, forgetting that the server was still at their table, waiting to take their drink order.

Eyes locked together, they picked up their menus and began perusing.

The rest of the night flew by in a haze of laughter and heart-shaped eyes. Gavin had never been on a date that flowed so well. It was as if his date could read his mind. They both enjoyed old romantic movies—anything with Meg Ryan and Tom Hanks. They preferred summer but loved a good white Christmas. And of course, they both loved puppies! Because, let’s face it, what kind of monster doesn’t love a good puppy?

“I still can’t believe we matched on a hookup app of all places,” Gavin remarked as he enjoyed the last of his chocolate dessert.

“And why is that so hard to believe?” Robert asked, leaning up on his elbows like Gavin was about to divulge some deep, dark secret.

“I don’t know. I just find that guys on those apps are only looking to fuck, and that’s it.”

"So why were you on there?" the brilliant doctor asked, eyes still locked on his.

Gavin stared at the man. He had a point.

"Well, like every other warm-blooded twenty-four-year-old, I get horny from time to time, and that night that we chatted, I was kind of... *horny*."

Gavin could feel his cheeks blush. It wasn't that he was embarrassed about sex or felt uncomfortable even talking about it. Quite the opposite. He loved sex. He loved dick and every damn inch of it.

He was just a little embarrassed at the moment because he was really fucking into this dude. Like head over heels, matching His and His towels.

"And what about now?" Robert asked, licking his bottom lip as his eyes lowered and fixed on Gavin's mouth.

Gavin was now licking the last of the chocolate syrup off his spoon, intentionally trying to get a rise out of the gentleman sitting across from him.

Dr. Robert Ashford was in his late thirties, perhaps early forties, and exuded confidence like Gavin had never seen.

There was something to be said about a man being confident. It instantly made Gavin's dick hard and his legs spread open. What could he say? He was a total bottom and loved it when a man took charge and made him his bitch.

"Now... *what*?" Gavin asked, teasing the man in front of him.

"Are you horny?"

Gavin's cock twitched behind his zipper. It was as if it were waiting for permission to leap forward and present itself.

Sliding his hand across the table, Gavin brushed his fingers along Robert's soft, perfectly manicured hands.

"I could go for a second dessert."

Smirking, the doctor raised his hand. "How about I get us the check?"

Cocky, it seemed, was another quality that added to the raging, hard pipe that was Gavin's dick.

Thirty minutes later, Gavin was in Robert's townhouse, sitting on his sofa, watching as the man fixed him a drink.

"I have to say, tonight was just... perfect," Gavin gushed as the doctor sat down next to him and passed him his drink.

"I couldn't agree more. Here's to a night you won't soon forget."

Gavin liked the sound of that.

They clinked their glasses together, then took a sip of their drinks.

Gavin was just about to lower his glass when Robert placed his fingers under it, encouraging him to drink more. It wasn't until Gavin had finished all the red wine in his glass that the doctor finally lowered his hand.

"Want another?" Robert asked, flashing him those dazzling baby-blue eyes of his.

So much for savoring the delicious flavor.

Gavin got the feeling that those powerful eyes could make anyone do anything he wanted. Even have another drink at the sexy stud's request.

Taking Gavin's glass, the good doctor didn't even wait for a response before heading to his minibar to freshen up their drinks.

What a gentleman.

The doctor freshened up their drinks, then took another seat beside him so they could continue their conversation.

Gavin couldn't believe how easy their conversations flowed. It was as if they had known each other for years.

"Here, let me refill that for you," he offered once again, taking his glass and walking over to the bar once more.

"Sure... I—" Gavin began before suddenly stopping.

Something wasn't right. He was beginning to feel a bit strange.

He was suddenly starting to feel a bit weird.

"I'm going to make myself another. These things always make me so thirsty," Robert noted without lifting his head.

His back was to Gavin as he began pouring himself a scotch.

The room around Gavin began to sway. He had been drunk before, many times, but this was something else entirely.

He was starting to feel drowsy and a tad bit woozy. *What the fuck was going on here?*

Gavin suddenly got a bad feeling in his gut.

Something was wrong.

Something just didn't feel right.

Slowly, he reached for the arm of the sofa, hoping to get to his feet, but missed and fell to the floor instead.

"*Tsk tsk*," he heard Robert say. "Looks like someone's had a little bit too much to drink."

This wasn't a case of having too much to drink; this was a case of someone slipping something into his drink!

He'd been roofied before. Thankfully, he'd had friends around to take care of him and make sure that he got home safe.

But now?

Now he was alone... in the house of a stranger... with no one here to help him.

Panic began to set in.

He spotted his empty wine glass sitting on the bar next to where the handsome doctor stood.

Why would a doctor spike his drink?

Why do you think? To get into those pants and do whatever the fuck he wants to you, that inner voice inside his head said.

He hated that voice. It always reminded him of all the stupid, idiotic things he had done in his life. Like going home with a complete stranger!

More panic.

He was having trouble keeping his eyes open.

He needed to get out!

He needed to get out of this house before... before he lost consciousness and the devastatingly handsome doctor decided to... do... whatever it was... that he was about to do.

That thought alone scared him.

Using all the strength Gavin could muster, he reached for the coffee table and managed to get up onto one knee.

He wasn't sure how long it had taken him, but by the time he managed to almost lift himself up, Robert Ashford was by his side.

"Gavin. Stop. You're only going to hurt yourself. Don't worry, I'll take real good care of you. I promise. I'll even leave you a heartfelt card when I'm all done with you."

Gavin's blood went cold.

Leave him a card?

Was he...?

"They don't call me the Valentine Killer for nothing."

Gavin's heart stopped.

The Valentine Killer?

Strong, warm arms wrapped themselves around Gavin's body.

His brain was so cloudy.

And... his body... Somehow, the doctor's hold felt so comfy and inviting, like all the world's troubles had magically disappeared and all that was left was this warm, fluffy pillow.

Gavin's eyes got heavy as the man behind him gently began to caress his face. His touch was so soft... so caring.

Nothing bad could possibly happen with someone so... gentle.

All he wanted to do was sleep...

His body was getting so heavy...

No. Fight! Don't give in to this monster's embrace, that inner voice inside him screamed.

This was now a matter of life and death!

He'd read about the Valentine Killer and what he did to his victims.

Gavin had never imagined that he might one day be one of those victims.

No! He was not giving in without a fight!

Forcing his eyes open, he reached across the coffee table. Reaching... searching... for anything he could find.

Gavin grabbed the first object his fingers came in contact with.

It was cold and solid. Probably one of those pretentious marble sculptures the man had sitting all around his house. One of those "I have money, so I'll spend it on fancy-ass crap that I don't need but looks fancy on display in my expensive-as-fuck Colorado townhouse" objects.

Whatever it was, he didn't care.

Wrapping his fingers tight around the object, he lifted it quickly and brought it down hard against the back of the doctor's head.

He heard an *umph* and watched as Robert's body dropped like an anvil.

Go! Now's your chance! that inner voice inside him screamed. *Run!*

With legs unstable and the world around him looking like it was underwater, Gavin ran toward the door and fumbled with the lock.

He let out a whimper as he fought against the fog that threatened to take over his mind.

His heart was pounding in his chest as his vision became blurry.

He struggled and fumbled with the lock, desperately trying to figure out how to unlock the damn door so he could escape before his body betrayed him and he passed out on the floor.

He needed to escape!

Finally, he heard a click. He had somehow managed to unlock the door.

He yanked it open and stumbled outside.

He wasn't sure what happened after that.

There were lights and sounds and people cursing at him.

He ran toward something large and solid. It had big flashing lights and looked so beautiful.

All he knew was that he needed to get to that peaceful object. If he could manage that, then he would be safe and happy.

If only...

The sound of loud screeching made Gavin jump, just

seconds before he felt something big and solid crash into his body.

He felt the wind across his skin before he landed on the cold, hard pavement below.

More screaming... and pounding.

Then...

The world around him suddenly went black.

2

MARCUS

Warm air surrounded Marcus as he stepped outside the back of his bar. *Ride 'em Hard* wasn't too busy tonight. Most customers tonight were locals, enjoying a pint or two before heading home to the Mrs.—or an empty house, depending on who you were.

It had been a long day, so Marcus decided to step outside for a bit and enjoy a cigar before heading home for the night.

He pulled a Cuban cigar out from his shirt pocket and used his clippers to snip off the end.

Memories of the first time he and the guys had tried to light a cigar came rushing back. They had been in their late teens and had no idea what the heck they were doing. They kept trying to light the cigar but couldn't understand why the damn thing wouldn't light.

It wasn't until one of the older guys caught them that

they discovered the secret to lighting a cigar was to snip the tip before trying to suck your brains out.

To add to Marcus's embarrassment, he tried to be all tough and macho by taking in deep puffs of smoke. All that ended up doing was causing him to choke and practically cough up a lung.

The guys got a good laugh out of that one.

Taking a deep breath, Marcus let the sweet and savory taste of the Cuban roll around on his tongue before slowly letting the smoke slip from his mouth.

Marcus wasn't a regular cigar smoker, but he liked to enjoy one from time to time.

Tonight, he'd run into an old buddy by the name of Eddy. They reminisced about old times and got caught up with what was new in each other's lives.

Marcus didn't really have much new going on in his life —not that he could really tell Eddy even if he did. Eddy, on the other hand, had gotten married a few years ago and now had two young daughters he was trying not to fuck up.

It was disturbing how quickly time flew by.

Marcus was no spring chicken. He was thirty-nine, going on sixty-two in gay years, as Ace liked to remind him... constantly. He was still single and didn't see that changing anytime soon.

In fact, he doubted that would ever change.

He didn't want a partner.

Spouses made you weak. They changed you. Made you

vulnerable in all the wrong places. Plus, they demanded way too much. It was like voluntarily having a probation officer move into your home just to monitor you and be a pain in your ass.

No thanks.

He didn't need someone questioning his whereabouts at all hours of the day. His business was his own, and no one else needed to know about it.

Sex? Well, he could get laid anytime he wanted. It's not like he had any trouble in that department. He just needed to unzip his fly, and people fell to their knees to service his cock.

He was the leader of the Shadow Vipers, a biker gang that dealt in weapons, drugs, and hard-to-find items. Women were always willing to drop to their knees for an alpha male. Especially one who was the leader of a rough and tough biker gang.

He was expanding his business westward and needed that to be his focus for the next few years.

Yup, relationships made people weak. They were a distraction and a nuisance, and he didn't have time for either.

Ace, his little brother—okay, stepbrother—had just gotten married to one of the other bikers in their crew.

Blade.

A pain in the ass, if there ever was one.

The douche was cocky, annoying, and a fucking horndog.

Every time Marcus saw his face, he wanted to bash it into the ground with his bare hand.

It had nothing to do with the fact that Blade was giving it to his little brother and everything to do with him being fucking annoying.

But thankfully, Ace and Blade had the good sense to move out of Marcus's house immediately after the wedding and purchase a place of their own—which happened to be only a few short blocks from his.

And no matter how much Ace tried to deny it, the thought of moving very far from Marcus scared him. Of course, Marcus would never call out his little brother on that. Truthfully, he felt exactly the same.

He loved his little brother, even if sometimes his overbearing nature showed the opposite. There wasn't anything he wouldn't do for the annoying little shit.

Taking another puff of his cigar, Marcus let the smoke drift from his lips as he let the peace around him calm his nerves.

Ahh, he loved a good cigar.

Now all he needed was a whiskey in one hand and a mouth wrapped around his cock.

That right there would be the perfect way to end an evening.

A ruffling in the bushes caught Marcus's attention.

Marcus shook his head.

These fucking guys...

"Which one of you idiots is back there getting your

dick sucked?" Marcus called out before sucking back another puff of his cigar and enjoying the flavor as it rolled around inside his mouth.

"Umm... me, boss?" Caden's voice answered from somewhere inside the bushes.

Marcus waited for a second.

"Umm... and me?" Lucas followed.

And there it was. Ride 'em Hard's horniest couple.

Marcus couldn't blame them. They were perfect for each other. Both madly in love with each other, both extremely jealous of the other.

Caden was one of Marcus's oldest friends, loyal to the end. When they were younger, he even did a few years behind bars in order to keep Marcus and Ace out of jail.

That was true friendship. That was true loyalty. Marcus could never repay that kind of debt. All he could do was spend his life showing Caden just how much he loved the guy.

Lucas, Caden's main squeeze and the other half of his heart, had stumbled into their lives just over a year ago. He had been running from an abusive ex, and let's just say that when Lucas's ex ended up finding him, that was the end of... his ex.

Marcus loved the kid. He made Caden happy, and that made Marcus happy. Sure, the guy might be a little unhinged when it came to bullies or people who tried to hurt him or his friends, but Lucas was pure sunshine. A smiling face and loving heart.

Since he could no longer enjoy his cigar while having to listen to Lucas suck Caden's cock, he decided to put the damn thing out and try again in about an hour. Hopefully, by then, no other members of his crew would be out here, trying to get their dicks sucked as well.

Whatever happened to fucking in the bathrooms?

"You boys can finish up. I'm heading back inside," Marcus grumbled, dabbing his cigar on the wall and then blowing off the last of the embers.

"Umm... thanks, boss. I owe you. Ow!" Caden cried out, after what Marcus could only imagine was Lucas slapping Caden's thigh. "What?"

"You owe him? What? Are you going to suck his dick too?"

More rustling from the bushes.

"Oh, don't be an idiot. You know what I meant," he heard Caden say as he signed his own death warrant.

Marcus chuckled as he went back inside.

He might not be in a relationship, but he knew it was never a good idea to call your partner an "idiot." That was the equivalent of throwing gasoline on an open fire.

He'd see them inside in a few minutes.

Chuckling, Marcus opened the back door, then headed into his office to finish up some paperwork.

He'd barely gotten the office door closed when his cell phone began to ring.

It was Sheriff Burke calling.

"Hey, Sheriff. How's the vacation?"

The sheriff and the Shadow Vipers had an unusual relationship. The sheriff allowed Marcus and his crew certain *liberties*—mainly, he turned a blind eye to Marcus's business—so long as it didn't draw attention to the town, and the Vipers helped keep the town of Baton, New Mexico, safe and violence-free.

Marcus applauded the sheriff's willingness to be accommodating and did what he could to respect his rules and keep the peace within the town. Baton was their home, after all, and they wanted nothing more than to be good, upstanding neighbors.

Currently, the sheriff was on vacation out in Colorado, helping a cousin of his who was also a sheriff and busy setting up his own task force to hunt a serial killer who had been active in the state for the past two years.

"Hey, Marcus, it's going fine. That's why I'm callin' actually."

The man sounded more stressed than he was before he left for his trip.

"What do you mean? What can I do for ya?" Marcus asked, not really sure how he could help the man relax.

"Look. I need a huge favor from you. I've got a kid down here who needs your protection."

"My protection?" Marcus asked, his interest suddenly piqued.

"Ya. You, as in, the Shadow Vipers. Look, this kid was almost murdered tonight, and I got a feeling it might have been the Valentine Killer who tried to kill him."

The Valentine murders were what the papers were calling the string of killings that had taken place over the past two years. The killer would leave a Valentine's card in the pocket of every victim, professing his undying love for them and promising to find them in the next life.

The victims were sexually assaulted first, before they had their throats slit and bodies dumped in a spot with some sort of romantic significance. The spots were always different, so it was difficult to predict where the next body would be found.

"Serious? No shit." Marcus couldn't believe it.

He'd been reading about the murders for the past year and couldn't believe that a potential victim actually escaped. He could only imagine how fucked up that person must be.

"Yeah, sure thing. What do you need us to do?"

"Thanks, Marcus. I owe you big time. Okay, I need you to drive down here and pick up the kid. Take him back to Baton and watch him. I think it's safer to get this kid out of the state in case the killer comes looking for him."

"And you don't think the police can do a better job of keeping this kid safe?" Marcus could barely get that out while keeping a straight face.

"Don't be a smart-ass. Who's going to come after a kid when he's got a whole goddamn biker gang protecting him?"

Burke was right. No man in his right mind would dare take on the Shadow Vipers. But a serial killer wasn't exactly in his right mind, was he? Was he really willing to put all their lives in danger just to protect some kid he didn't even know?

"Marcus, you still there?" Burke's voice cut through his train of thought.

"Yeah, man. Pick up the kid. Protect the kid. Prove that cops can't do shit." Marcus gave a snort as he added that last part.

"I seem to remember saving your ass a few times over the years. If I'm not mistaken, I think the last one involved that boy Lucas, a bunch of snakes, and one dead ex. Am I right?"

Damn, motherfucker.

"So, it seems that I owe you... *a few*," Marcus noted. "Send me the address, and I'll head out tomorrow morning, boss."

"Thanks, Marcus. I knew I could count on you and your boys for help."

They ended their call. Marcus sat in silence, gripping his phone in his hand as he stared off into space.

The police had a witness now. He wondered how long it would take before this motherfucker was caught. The thought of someone preying on lovesick men, whose only crime was that they were hoping to find their forever partner, made him sick.

For now, he would take in this kid and provide him with the best fucking protection known to man.

No, Marcus was not cocky at all.

3

MARCUS

It was about a six-hour drive from Baton, New Mexico, to Colorado Springs, where Burke was keeping the kid in police custody.

Marcus had borrowed Alexis and Jake's car, figuring it would be easier to smuggle a kid out of a police station in a car than on the back of a motorcycle. Plus, Marcus wasn't sure how good the kid would be on the back of a bike for six hours, clinging to a complete stranger. He might feel weird or uncomfortable.

Stepping out of the car, Marcus stretched his back and winced. He needed to start taking more breaks on long drives because his back was no longer twenty years old. While he still hit the gym five days a week and was as large as a tank, the truth was that nature was starting to catch up to him. But there was no way in hell he was letting any of the guys know that.

No. He kept pushing them hard at the gym to prove to the guys that he still had control and could be relied on to lead. Nobody wanted to be led by a biker who had back problems and whose knees cracked whenever he got up—which they did.

Fuck, getting older sucked.

Marcus had left Baton around six a.m., so it was just after noon when he arrived at the police station.

Burke had decided that after the kid was checked out by the doctors, the next safest place for him was the police station. So he had him tucked away in one of the cells, where at least six officers could keep an eye on him.

Once Marcus stepped into the station, the officer behind the front desk glanced up and gave Marcus a head-to-toe. He wasn't sure whether the woman was impressed by the hotness of his swollen muscles or by the size of his six-foot-four, tatted frame.

Perhaps she was wondering whether someone had left a cell unlocked, and Marcus was kindly returning himself after taking a leisurely morning stroll.

Either way, he'd take the compliment.

"How can I help you?" the woman finally asked once she was done eye-fucking Marcus.

Marcus placed his hands on the counter and began tapping his fingers on the surface.

"I'm here to see Sheriff Burke. Name's Marcus."

"Marcus!" a voice shouted from down the hall.

The woman pointed over her shoulder to where Burke

was standing next to an office door, signaling for him to come in.

"Thanks," Marcus said, giving the woman a nod as he walked around the counter and into the "Police Only" restricted area.

"Marcus, thanks for coming," Sheriff Burke greeted, patting Marcus on the back as he entered the office. Another man was already seated behind the desk. "Please, have a seat." Burke motioned to the empty chair sitting in front of the large, cluttered desk. "This here is my cousin, Quaid. Officer Pike, if you will."

The officer behind the desk leaned forward and offered Marcus his hand. "It's a pleasure to meet you, and thanks for coming."

Marcus took a seat, just as the officer from the front desk entered, carrying a coffee for Marcus.

"Umm, thanks," Marcus offered, taking the mug from the woman and setting it down on the desk.

The two other men in the room looked up at her, mouths slightly open.

"You two can get your own damn coffee," she said before exiting the room.

Marcus let out a snort.

Officer Pike huffed, then fixed a few of the papers that were thrown across his desk.

"Whatever. Look. I'm grateful that you're willing to do this and help us out, but as I've mentioned to my cousin, I'm not exactly keen on having a criminal organization protecting one of our witnesses. What kind of message would that send?"

Marcus sat up and leaned forward.

"Criminal organization?" Marcus asked, pressing his arm against the man's desk as he studied his face more closely. "To which crimes are you accusing my club of participating in?"

The man's eyes went wide when it finally sank in just how big Marcus really was.

"Look. We both know that you're selling more than just booze down in that sleepy little town my cousin likes to call home, but I'm serious when I say, the media will have a shitstorm when they find out that one of our witnesses is being protected by *The Mountain* and his biker gang."

Marcus wasn't sure how he felt about being compared to the large beast of a man in *Game of Thrones*, especially since his face was all burned to shit. Was the man calling him ugly? Or just big and scary?

"I thought the whole point of this was to make sure that nobody—the press included—finds out where this kid is hiding? Trust me, serial killer or not, nobody is going to try and get to this kid with a bunch of scary biker dudes standing guard, protecting him," Marcus growled back.

Sheriff Burke smirked. "My thoughts exactly."

He sat his ass down on the edge of his cousin's desk and crossed his arms against his chest.

"From what we know so far, the kid was on a date with the guy, then went back to his place for a bit of fun. The bastard drugged him, then tried to force himself onto him. The kid fought back and managed to escape. He's lucky. He could have been victim number seven if he hadn't managed to get away."

"So, the kid knows where the killer lives?" Marcus asked. "Why aren't you there arresting him?"

"That's the problem. The kid was so drugged up, he doesn't remember escaping or where the guy actually lives. He gave us a description of the guy, but it's pretty generic. Black hair, blue eyes, strong jaw. He gave us a name as well, Robert Ashford, but we aren't even sure if that's a real name. He said he was a plastic surgeon, but we can't find a Dr. Ashford anywhere in Colorado or neighboring states."

"So basically, you got shit," Marcus huffed, leaning back in his chair and picking up his cup of coffee. He gave it a blow before taking a sip.

What a bunch of fucking morons.

"We have a team reviewing video surveillance to retrace the kid's steps. Even if we find this guy's address, he's probably long gone since someone can now ID him," Burke's cousin added.

"What we need right now is for you to keep this kid safe and out of harm's way while we search for this bastard," Burke continued. "Do you think you can do that?"

Marcus locked eyes with the sheriff. While he liked to bust the guy's balls, he wasn't a monster. Of course he would help protect the kid—even if he had no interest in being a glorified babysitter.

"On one condition."

"Oh? And what's that?" Officer Pike asked, locking his fingers together as he waited.

"Even when this is all said and done, there's no mention that my crew and I helped you out with this investigation." Marcus stood. "We got a reputation to keep, and helping lazy cops like yourself would make us look weak."

Sheriff Burke smirked. "I think we can arrange that."

"Good! Now let's go see your kid," Officer Pike announced, getting up from his desk and walking around to where Marcus was waiting. "Right this way."

They walked down the hallway and through a locked corridor until they came to a row of single jail cells. Some cells were occupied, while others stood empty.

Marcus followed the sheriff and his cousin to the very last cell, where a young man lay on a bench, his arm thrown over his eyes, his legs bent at the knees, apparently enjoying a nap.

"It's time to wake up, *Sleeping Beauty*," Officer Pike announced, placing his key in the metal slot and turning it until the cell unlocked.

A groan came from the man, whose body barely moved an inch.

"First, you stick me in this hideous outfit, then you refuse to leave me in peace. Since when is the victim of a psychopathic murderer locked up in jail and held without bail?" The young man threw his legs over the side of the bench and sat up in one smooth motion.

The young man was pretty, in that Disney prince sort of way. His hair was dark, but his eyes were as blue as the waters in Fiji.

His lips were smooth and perfect, with just enough plump to turn those bad boys into dick-sucking machines if given the right opportunity.

There was something about the way the boy was sitting, mouthing off to those in authority—not taking shit—that was kind of giving Marcus a chubby.

He liked the boy's sass. His sarcasm and defiance. It made him want to bend the boy over his lap and teach the little prick a lesson.

"Oh! You brought friends," the fairy-tale prince announced, jumping from his seat and flashing them all his biggest smile.

Marcus half expected woodland creatures to appear and start singing. Perhaps a mouse or two would pull out some fabric and start designing a new outfit for his highness.

"Gavin, this here is Marcus. He'll be taking care of you for a while," Officer Pike explained, pointing at Marcus with his thumb.

"Taking care of me? Well, hello, Daddy!" the boy said with a boost of enthusiasm that was not lost on anyone in the cell.

Marcus took a step forward, crossing his arms over his

chest, and glared at the bouncing boy. It was important to assert dominance over your subject early in the relationship.

"Think of me as your jailer. You'll be under my custody for the next several weeks. I am God to you. Whatever I say, goes. Is that understood?"

Gavin's eyes dilated.

"Big, strong, and bossy. Damn, I like this one, Officer P.," Gavin exclaimed with a mischievous smirk on his face.

This one was going to be trouble.

"You'll be staying with Marcus until we're able to locate and arrest the man who attacked you," Sheriff Burke explained.

The light from the boy's eyes suddenly dimmed, and the once flirty and cheery prince had suddenly vanished.

"I don't need protecting. What I need is to get the fuck out of this cell, then go home, shower, and jerk off." He locked eyes with Marcus. "You can always come join me in the shower if you want, *Mr. Mountain Man*. I'm great at giving back rubs."

Marcus glanced over at Burke. "Are we done here?"

The man nodded.

"Good," Marcus said, stepping into the cell and grabbing Gavin by his hips. He then tossed the startled boy over his shoulder without warning—or effort.

"Hey! What the fuck?" Gavin screamed, clinging to Marcus's shirt as he hung upside down over his shoulder.

"Can you grab the door for me, please?" Marcus asked

Officer Pike, who was looking at him with wide eyes and a gaping mouth.

Marcus stepped out into the hallway and began heading toward the front door.

"Hello? Police? Does anyone see this man kidnapping me and forcing me to leave with him against my will?" Gavin called out to the dozen or so smiling faces who stood back and watched as Marcus walked with him through the precinct and out the front door.

A few officers outside glanced at them briefly, appearing to wonder if they should intervene. That is, until they spotted Officers Burke and Pike shaking their heads.

Apparently, kidnapping was okay, so long as your bosses gave you the all-clear.

"Let me go, you behemoth gorilla!" the boy yelled.

He began pounding his fists against Marcus's back, which only made things so much funnier. It was like having his own personal masseuse massaging his sore back muscles, getting him ready for the long ride home. He could get used to such premium service.

Stopping at his car, Marcus fished the keys from his pocket and popped open the trunk.

"Oh, you've got to be kidding me," Gavin argued the moment he spotted the open trunk. "Don't you d—" Gavin landed with a thud into the bottom of the trunk.

"Enjoy the ride," Marcus said with a smirk as he

slammed the hood down, nearly decapitating his newest passenger.

Fists pounded, and screaming ensued, all to Marcus's smirking pleasure. He was so glad he agreed to this gig. It was going to be so much fun.

“Umm, sir? Is that a person in your trunk?” a pimply-faced, new recruit asked sheepishly as he nodded toward Marcus’s trunk.

“Oh, don't worry, this is just one of our kinky little sex games."

“No, it’s not! The man is trying to abduct me! I heard him say something about having a micropenis, and this was his way of seeking vengeance on all of us well-hung twinks! The man is deranged! Please let me out!”

Marcus leaned forward as if trying to hear what the young man was saying.

"What’s that? Sorry, but I can't hear you, babe. Try removing that ball gag from your mouth and speaking clearly, sweet pea."

“Argh! You’re such a fucking asshole!” the young man screamed.

“See, everything’s good, here, Officer,” Marcus noted, smiling at the man as he rounded the car. He gave Burke and Pike a wave as he got into the driver’s side.

Once inside, he turned up the music and reveled in the tortured curses of his newest assignment.

4

GAVIN

Seething, Gavin braced himself for another impact of his head against the top of the hood. It had been like this for the last ten minutes. It seemed like his kidnapper, Megatron in the flesh, had decided to take the scenic route and hit every bump and pothole there was in Colorado.

Like, seriously? Where the fuck were they?

Gavin jerked forward when the car suddenly came to a complete stop. He heard the engine die and the car door open and close.

This was it. The bastard was finally coming to let him out.

He pulled the crowbar closer to his body and gripped the end with all the strength he had. How could the police let him be taken by this Cro-Magnon of a human? The man was all brute force and minimal intelligence.

“Hope you’re still alive in there,” a deep voice said as the world was suddenly filled with light.

Gavin let out a scream and drew the crowbar down hard on the man who had kidnapped him.

“What the—” Marcus began as the crowbar hit his bicep with absolutely no pain.

Gavin looked at the monstrous bicep and gasped. “What the hell? Not even an ouch or cry of pain?”

Marcus looked at his arm and shrugged.

“Was that supposed to hurt or something?”

“That was supposed to knock you unconscious and scramble your brain, giving me time to climb out of this car and escape,” Gavin screeched, flustered and a bit annoyed.

Marcus looked down at the boy.

“Do you want me to lie down now and pretend to be knocked unconscious? I can even roll around and moan if that makes you feel better.”

Gavin just glared at the annoying man.

“You’re freakishly large, you know that?”

Marcus gave him a smirk. “No one’s ever complained about how large I am before. Never thought that would be an issue.”

Gavin stared at him once more, trying to figure out whether the man was friend or foe. Smart or dumb. Straight or…

“Do you want to come sit up front with me now? No

one's been following us," Marcus said, holding out his hand.

No one's been following us? What the fuck did that mean?

Letting out a breath, Gavin raised both his arms and let the ogre lift him from the trunk. Being with a mountain of a man definitely had its perks.

Once they were back in the car, Marcus passed him a bottle of water. "Here, drink this. You must be thirsty."

Gavin snatched the bottle and began chugging. Not because he was thirsty, but because he didn't want his kidnapper to have any. Yes, that was what he told himself.

"We'll stop for food in about an hour. I just want to get us out of the area so nobody recognizes you."

"What do you mean? Who would recognize me?"

"The killer. The police haven't arrested him yet, and he might still be out there looking to finish the job."

Gavin's heart stopped in his chest. He hadn't even thought about the killer coming back to finish the job. He just figured the killer would take off and run before the police could find him. But now...

Gavin looked out his window and subconsciously leaned toward Marcus.

"Don't worry. No one saw you leave the precinct. You're safe with me now, peanut."

"What do you mean, 'no one saw us'? Everyone at the precinct saw you kidnap me gorilla-style and throw me into your trunk," Gavin barked, convinced that the man was mad.

"Yes, everyone saw me carrying a screaming twink back to my car. If you ask anyone, all they will remember seeing is some big, scary biker dude carrying some screaming twink over his shoulder and dumping that kid in the trunk of his car. They won't be able to tell you anything about the kid, except that he was annoying when he screamed."

Gavin stared at him, dumbfounded.

"So, all of that aggressive kidnapping was just for show?"

"Hey, I had to get you out of there somehow. Plus, it felt really good throwing you in my trunk, then driving circles over pebbled road." Marcus gave him a smirk.

"You're an asshole, you know?"

"Yes, I've been told that from time to time," Marcus agreed with a shit-eating grin plastered to his face. They proceeded back to the highway.

Gavin kept eyeing the hulking beast currently kidnapping/not kidnapping him. Somehow, this man had been assigned as his protector. He didn't know who the guy was or how he ended up in his orbit. But one thing was certain, Gavin wanted to ride that cowboy till he couldn't see straight.

Reaching over to the radio, Gavin began playing around with the stations.

A big meaty paw grabbed his hand and tossed it aside.

"Rule number one: Don't touch anything. This isn't my car, and I don't want you fucking up any of Alexis's preset stations."

Gavin gave him side-eye.

"Is Alexis your girlfriend?"

Marcus let out a growl. "Mind your business."

Gavin let out a huff. "We're going to be rubbing up against each other for the next few weeks, so we should probably kinda get to know each other."

"There will be no rubbing," Marcus commanded.

"Okay, fine. Cuddling if you prefer." Gavin let out a chuckle when Marcus glared at him.

"So? Who's Alexis?"

"One of the bartenders who works at my bar."

"So, not a girlfriend."

Marcus just growled.

"Okay. And why is it that you have her car and not your own? You broke or something?"

Judging by the biker leather jacket the man was wearing and the designer jeans he had on, Gavin was pretty sure he was not lacking money. Plus, his boots alone cost close to a thousand bucks!

"No, I'm not broke. I borrowed Alexis's car because I figured it would be easier for you to drive six hours in a car, instead of strapped to the back of my Harley, holding my waist."

Gavin's eyes lit up.

"Oh no, dear. Option number one would have worked perfectly. Six hours cuddled up against you is every gay boy's wet dream."

Marcus glanced over at Gavin but remained silent.

Was the man homophobic?

"You got something against queers?" Gavin fumed. Subtlety was never his strong suit.

Letting out something that sounded rather like annoyance, Marcus glanced over at Gavin as he drove.

"Just because I don't want to be cuddling up against you doesn't make me homophobic. I'm more 'annoying-twink phobic.' Plus, my brother is gay, and so is his husband, Blade—who I often threaten with shooting him in the face, but that's because he is annoying and sticking it to my brother. Then there is Caden, my oldest friend, who just decided he liked dick when he met Lucas, a feisty little twink who's more murderous than should be legal. Then there is Nikolai, our scary Russian, who recently decided he was committing to his longtime best friend and trying out monogamy.

"So, no. I'm not homophobic. My biker bar is becoming a sausage fest and smells like cock and cum on Friday and Saturday nights. Don't ask me why that is. But I suspect Ace and Blade have something to do with it. Maybe even Caden and Lucas."

Gavin sat staring at him, his mouth wide open and his skin buzzing with excitement.

"You own a biker bar? Wait! Are you in some kind of biker gang? Is that why the sheriff wanted you to protect me? Am I being protected by *Sons of Anarchy*?" He slapped his leg and bounced around in his seat.

Marcus shook his head. "You're an idiot. Let's stop in here for some lunch."

They pulled into a roadside diner, and Marcus wasted no time in hopping out and barreling toward the door.

Gavin was quick on his heels.

"So, tell me, what position do you hold in this biker gang hierarchy? Like, are you the enforcer man? The weapons guy? The *cleaner*?" Gavin raised his eyebrow at that last one. He wasn't sure how excited he should be about traveling across the state with a man who could make a person disappear.

Marcus held open the door and pushed Gavin through by placing his hand at the back of his neck and giving him a herculean shove.

"I'm the guy at the top of the food chain," Marcus said with a hint of danger in his voice.

Gavin stopped suddenly, causing his back to bounce off Marcus's abnormally large chest.

"Wait. You're the leader of the biker gang?" His mind was blown. "Why the fuck would the leader drive all this way to pick up my sorry ass?"

Marcus pushed Gavin into an empty seat. "Sit." His jailer circled the table and sat across from him. "I came to get you because Sheriff Burke, a friend, asked me to protect you. I also heard about the murders and wanted to check things out myself."

The waitress came over and dropped menus on the

table for them to check. Once the waitress had taken their order, she disappeared into the back.

"Are you sure you only want a salad and steamed vegetables for lunch? Aren't you hungry?" Marcus asked, leaning back in his chair and giving him a perplexed look.

"I'm actually a vegetarian."

Marcus's mouth stiffened. "A what?"

"A vegetarian."

Marcus shook his head. "A veg...?"

Frustrated, Gavin let out a breath. "It's when a person doesn't eat meat. They value life and don't want to consume animal carcasses."

Marcus began to chuckle. "I know what a vegetarian is, preachy."

Gavin's eyes narrowed. The man was infuriating.

The elderly couple sitting next to them turned and gawked at Gavin.

"Sorry, my friend here is a little passionate about Bambi. I'll try to keep his preachiness under control," Marcus whispered to the elderly couple.

"You're still an ass," Gavin noted.

Marcus shrugged.

5

MARCUS

Because nothing is ever secret when it comes to the Shadow Vipers, Marcus wasn't surprised to see Lucas and Ace sitting on the front steps when he and Gavin pulled into his driveway.

Throwing the car into park, Marcus let out a growl as if that would chase off the pests currently lingering around, trying to act all innocent and not like the *Nosy Housewives of Baton, New Mexico.*

"What are you idiots doing here?" Marcus asked as he opened the car door and stepped out.

Ace looked up, startled, as if he hadn't noticed the gray, beat-up car that had just pulled up into the driveway of his old house.

"Oh! Hey, big brother. What are you doing home? I thought you had... oh!" Ace stood and slapped his forehead as if he had just remembered something. "I forgot, you had the thing... with the guy... in the place."

Rounding the car, Marcus nodded at his idiotic brother and the ever-smiling little elf currently standing behind Ace.

"Gavin, this is Ace, my nosy gay brother, and his side-kick, *Sir Sucks Dick-a-Lot.*"

"Also known as Lucas," Lucas said, stepping forward and offering his hand. "Is it true you're going to be staying with this ogre for the foreseeable future?" Lucas asked, still keeping Ace a safe distance between him and Marcus.

"And also, why am I introduced as the 'gay' brother?" Ace asked as if he were annoyed by the colorful introduction.

Marcus walked past Ace and Lucas, nodding for Gavin to follow him.

"Oh, I accused him of being homophobic earlier, so he's trying to prove to me that he does in fact have a gay brother, and a gay brother's gay best friend, and a whole other queer ensemble."

Ace chuckled. "Please. Once, someone called me a faggot in high school, and Marcus and his friends kicked the shit out of the guy. Did he tell you I'm married to one of his best friends?" Ace asked, throwing his arm around Gavin's shoulder while Lucas linked his arm through Gavin's. The three walked up the walkway, looking like the *Lollipop Guild* on its way to visit Dorothy.

"And I told him how much I want to shoot Blade in the

face, which has nothing to do with the dick-sucking," Marcus grumbled as he entered the house.

"He's still adjusting to the whole 'friend fucking his little bro' thing," he heard Ace say to Gavin outside.

"Can you please get inside before someone sees you. You're supposed to be hiding out, remember?" Marcus barked.

"Ooh," Ace and Lucas chirped as they picked up their pace, sandwiching Gavin between them.

It was just after seven p.m., so it was time to start making something for dinner.

What do vegetarians eat?

He didn't have any rabbit food, and the last of his lettuce died a tragic death in the bottom of his crisper.

Seriously, why do people use that damn thing? It's basically a portal to another dimension where food disappears once you buy it, then magically reappears months later, brown, sad, and missing a life force.

He needed to stop buying lettuce. He always had good intentions of eating healthier, but let's be honest, his diet mainly consisted of chicken, steak, and protein shakes. Oh, and whiskey.

What more did a solid biker need?

"Okay, I don't have any plant food here, but I can order us a pizza with... what? Tomatoes? Grapes? Cucumbers? What do vegetarians put on their disgusting pizza?" Marcus asked, pulling his cell from his back pocket.

"How about you dial, and I'll place the order?" Gavin offered, giving him a knowing smile.

"Sure. Order me an all-meat pizza, large, and whatever these nosy Bettys want to eat."

The gossip queens cheered as Marcus went to the bar to fix them all a few drinks. Ace and Lucas would want their sangrias. *Damn. For that, he would need to head to the kitchen.*

An hour later, they were plowing through the pizzas and halfway through their second pitcher of sangria, with Marcus enjoying his whiskey.

"Okay, so give us the details. Who are you, and what's going on?" Ace asked, sitting cross-legged on the floor as he looked up at Gavin, who was sitting on the couch next to Lucas.

"Gavin, you don't need to disclose anything you don't want to. I'm here to protect you. You don't owe us anything." Marcus jumped in before Gavin could start.

Ace gave his brother a dirty look.

"There isn't much to tell. As your brother said, he's here to protect me and keep me safe from some serial killer who is trying to murder me."

Both Ace's and Lucas's mouths dropped open. They stared at Gavin without saying a word.

"We. Need. More. Information," Ace said, jumping up from the floor and squeezing between Lucas and Gavin.

Marcus tried not to laugh.

"Okay, okay, start from the beginning," Ace gushed,

linking his arm through Gavin's and staring at him like they were on some kind of daytime talk show.

Gavin glanced over at Marcus, who just shrugged his shoulders.

"Well, this guy asked me out and took me to this fancy restaurant I love, called Restaurante Piccolo. Everything started off so normal. He was nice, attentive, and we had so much in common."

"Except for the murder thing, I'm guessing?" Lucas jumped in.

Gavin nodded with a half smile. "After dinner, we went back to his place, and that's when everything changed. He drugged my wine, then attacked me. He basically told me that he was the Valentine Killer and that he was going to murder me."

Ace and Lucas both gasped, throwing their hands over their mouths and looking like they had just lived through the ordeal themselves.

"Oh my god! Are you okay?" they both asked, reaching for Gavin and giving him a supportive squeeze.

"Easy there, big guys," Marcus said. "The guy's fine. He's a fighter. And now he's here with us, under the protection of the Shadow Vipers."

"Yes! That's right. My brother's crew will protect you and keep you safe," Ace added.

"We'll find this motherfucker and end his ass!" Lucas finished off with.

Okay, things were starting to spiral here.

"Alright, my little fighter cranes, there will be no hunting of the serial killer and definitely no ending of his ass. We are on protection detail only. The Colorado Police have their very own task force and are looking into the matter as we speak. Hopefully, they will have the guy in custody in a few days. Then Gavin can go back to his old life, and Lucas can stop thinking of ways to murder people."

"God, when did your brother become such a stiff?" Lucas asked Ace as if he wasn't even in the room.

Shaking his head, Marcus stood.

"As far as the rest of the Vipers know, Gavin is just a witness the sheriff has asked us to protect. We don't want people in town knowing that he's connected to the Valentine murders, so keep that info to yourselves."

Marcus looked at both Ace and Lucas, who both looked like they had swallowed a canary.

The little shits.

"This means not telling Blade or Caden. Got it?" Marcus growled.

"You want us to lie to our significant others?" Ace asked, acting all dramatic and shocked to his core.

"You're not lying. You're following a direct order from your leader." Marcus gave him a smirk. He knew the argument was now over. He rarely played the "I'm the leader" card, but when he did, he expected absolute obedience.

Ace's mouth dropped open. "You. Bastard."

"Same goes for you, Lucas."

The man nodded without making eye contact.

The weakling would fold the second he got home to Caden.

It was time for bed.

"Gavin, your bedroom is at the end of that hallway. It's Ace's old room. Ace, Lucas, you're welcome to stay the night here on the couch or go home to your husbands or whatever you call them. I don't care. I'm going to bed. Good night, Gavin."

"Good night, Marcus. And thanks for everything today."

That caught Marcus off guard. He'd been expecting something a little more sarcastic, like "Thank you for kidnapping me today," or perhaps, "Eat my ass and die, asshole." That seemed a bit more appropriate than a sincere thank-you.

"It's no problem at all," Marcus huffed, refusing to turn around and acknowledge the boy's kindness. He continued on to his room.

6

GAVIN

Gavin hadn't been able to sleep a wink. Every twenty minutes, he kept tossing and turning. It wasn't that he wasn't tired. Quite the opposite, he was exhausted. But every time he closed his eyes, he kept seeing *him*, standing over him with that eerie smile on his face as he promised to write him a romantic Valentine's card when he decided to end his life.

Each time he saw that face, his eyes jerked open, and his heart started pounding until he finally decided that he wasn't going to get any more sleep tonight.

Slipping out of his bed, he stepped into the living room and stared at his two new best friends—both sleeping on the floor on a bed made of pillows.

Lucas and Ace had decided that a sleepover was warranted so they could spend more time getting to know their newest best friend.

Gavin kind of liked that thought—having two best friends.

While Gavin might have 1.8 million followers across all his social media platforms, he didn't really have anyone he considered a "best friend" or even a close friend he could turn to for support or even help following such a traumatic experience.

Instead, he had a bunch of faceless profiles, all wanting a piece of him, all worshipping the ground he walked on. And for what? Because they liked the content he was posting and the recommendations he was making. Becoming a social media influencer was a gift and also a curse. It took a lot of hard work to constantly create content and keep producing work that people wanted to see.

Sometimes he felt like his whole life was one big performance.

Tiptoeing through the living room, he looked at the photos that hung on the walls. Most were of Marcus and Ace, smiling together, surrounded by big, beefy bikers who seemed to always be celebrating one occasion or another.

They all seemed happy, every person in those photos.

There were no scowls or rolling eyes, no disappointed parents or empty chairs at birthdays. All the pictures showed a loving life surrounded by people who cared.

Not wanting to wake the guys, Gavin moved on to the hallway.

Marcus's bedroom was located at the other end of the

long, ranch-style home, presumably to give a bit of privacy between the two brothers when they lived together.

Ace mentioned that Marcus had bought the place from their stepparents and then remodeled the rooms to make the bedrooms bigger and more accessible to their lifestyle.

As Gavin continued down the hallway, his eyes were fixed on the bedroom door at the end. Most people closed their bedroom doors when they went to sleep, but it appeared that Marcus had left his open.

Did he just forget to close his door? Or was this Marcus's way of reminding his family that he was always accessible, even when sleeping?

Gavin's parents were never like that. They believed in boundaries and in being appropriate, never showing too much emotion or inconveniencing others when you could do something yourself. They were both CEOs of major marketing firms and believed that hugging children was a sign of weakness.

Was it any surprise that Gavin would seek out attention and approval wherever he could get it? Anonymous adoration as a social media influencer felt just as good as having hundreds of friends.

Gavin stopped just outside Marcus's bedroom.

Jesus. His breath caught in his chest when his eyes fell on Marcus.

The man was lying on his stomach, his body spread out on the bed. His back muscles were exposed, taunting Gavin with every movement.

His eyes slid down his body, where a sheet was lazily thrown over his lower torso, leaving his left ass cheek partially exposed. Thankfully, he was wearing a pair of black cotton boxer briefs. If he weren't, Gavin was pretty sure the bedroom doorframe would be covered in his cum right this very second.

Talk about a sexy beefcake. The man was hairy in all the right places—his legs, his face, even his forearms. But his back was smooth, covered in muscles and tattoos that only added to Gavin's growing obsession with the mystery man.

There was something about a big, rough man that always made Gavin weak in the knees.

Yes, he'd slept with twinks, gym bunnies, and bears and chubs—hey, a dick was a dick, and a mouth was a mouth. He loved all body types, but his weakness was big, muscled daddies who liked being rough with their boys.

Instant hard-on.

The sound of Marcus's soft snoring was gentle and peaceful—almost like a lullaby. For some strange reason, Gavin felt a sense of comfort listening to Marcus sleep and knowing that the big badass was only steps away.

He wasn't trying to be creepy. He was just so goddamn tired, and the rhythmic sound of Marcus's snoring made Gavin's eyes get heavy.

Before he knew it, he found his body slowly sliding down the wall until he was seated on the floor, his back pressed against the wall, knees tucked up under his arms.

He rested his head against his knees and closed his eyes for just a moment.

A second later, he felt someone gently kick his foot.

Gavin jerked awake, his head snapping up to meet a pair of gentle brown eyes. His six-foot-four protector stared down at him.

"Did you get any sleep at all?" Marcus asked, staring down at him in nothing but his underwear. His chest had a light dusting of fur that hugged the perfectly sculpted curves of his pecs.

Without realizing it, Gavin's eyes slowly slid lower to the eight-pack the mountain man had somehow managed to obtain.

"Jesus" slipped out of Gavin's mouth before his eyes snapped back up to the smirking man standing above him.

"You checking out my junk, boy?"

Gavin hadn't even thought about that. He'd been too distracted by the miles of muscle scorching his eyeballs. So, of course, his eyes naturally dropped to the massive bulge barely being supported by the thin material that mere mortals call underwear.

A snort escaped Marcus's throat.

Gavin felt his cheeks flush.

"Uh—sorry." He waited for his brain to come back online. "Jesus. Your muscles have muscles. Do you live at the gym or something?" Gavin asked, hopping up from the floor and nearly kissing Marcus's bulge with the side of his face.

Another flash of crimson.

"I like to stay in shape," Marcus said, returning to his room and stepping into a pair of joggers he'd thrown on the floor.

Gavin followed him into his bedroom.

"So, you didn't answer my question. Did you get any sleep?" Marcus asked once again.

Shrugging his shoulders, Gavin sat down on Marcus's bed.

"I guess at some point? Every time I closed my eyes, I kept seeing his smirking face staring at me. I kept hearing him say not to worry, he was going to leave me a really romantic Valentine's card when he killed me. I finally gave up trying to sleep and decided to snoop around your house instead. Strangely enough, it was the sound of your snoring that finally made me fall asleep."

Marcus threw a shirt over his head and managed to squeeze his arms through the tiny holes.

"Well, I guess that makes sense. You see me as your big, strong protector. So it's only natural that you would feel comfortable sleeping when you're around me."

"So does that mean I get to cuddle with you at night?" Gavin's eyes lit up, and his smile nearly swallowed his head.

"Nice try. I'll get you a doll and slap a picture of me on its face. You can cuddle that instead."

Disappointment set in as Gavin's fantasies of being

swallowed alive by Marcus's swollen body evaporated before his eyes.

Gavin let out a sigh. "Fine... You're no fun." He looked up at Marcus, then back at the door. "Do you think they saw me sleeping outside your doorway, like a neglected little puppy?"

Marcus glanced at the door, then shook his head. "No, those gossip queens won't open their eyes until at least noon. Something about beauty sleep and them not being spring chickens anymore."

"Don't let them hear you say that." Gavin chuckled. There was something calming and relaxing about Marcus. He felt like no matter what, he could be himself around the big, burly man.

Placing his hand on Gavin's shoulder, Marcus led him out of his bedroom and into the kitchen.

"So, what do you want for breakfast? I guess you don't eat eggs," Marcus noted, scouring the fridge as he tried to figure out what vegetarians eat for breakfast.

Gavin couldn't help but smile.

7

MARCUS

"So, is it true?" Caden asked the second Marcus walked into the back of the bar.

"Is what true?" he asked, dropping a box of supplies onto the table.

"That you are babysitting a Valentine murder victim?"

Marcus glanced up at Caden and gave him a look.

"How could I be babysitting somebody who's dead?"

Caden looked at him, confused and trying to figure out what he got wrong.

"But Lucas said…" he began before realizing what he was about to admit to.

"Lucas has a big mouth," Marcus said, turning back to the box he had just brought in. He began unloading boxes of straws and putting them in a pile for Damien to take to the front of the bar whenever he had a chance.

"So? Is it true?" Caden asked once again, this time leaning against one of the tables in the back.

Marcus broke up the empty box and then laid it flat on the table. He gave Caden a stern look, then double-checked that no one else was around to overhear.

"Yes, what Lucas said is true. Sheriff Burke asked us to watch and protect Gavin until they can catch this mother-fucker and Gavin can testify. I need you to keep this info to yourself. The fewer people who know the truth, the better."

Blade decided to walk into the back room at that very moment.

Both Marcus and Caden froze, watching Blade as he cautiously came to a stop a few steps from the door.

"Yes, I know all about our special guest. And no, I didn't ask Ace to blab his mouth." He continued walking toward the basement, then disappeared from sight.

Marcus shook his head. "I swear to god, nobody follows orders anymore."

A few seconds later, Ace, Lucas, and Gavin all walked into the back laughing before they came to a sudden halt.

"What?" Ace asked, shrugging his shoulder as if he hadn't a clue what all the whispering was about.

"You and I are going to have a talk about what following orders means," Marcus growled.

"Now, now, Daddy, it's too early to be this growly," Gavin interjected.

Shaking his head, he pointed at Gavin. "You. Come with me," he said as he walked toward the basement door.

Gavin looked at Ace and Lucas, who both shrugged at him.

"Now," Marcus barked, walking down the stairs. Gavin came running after him like a good little puppy.

Wow, what's all this? Gavin asked, looking at the heaps of merchandise that had fallen off trucks in recent months.

Some items were spoken for, while others were for the Vipers to use whenever they... needed something.

Other items, like the leather jackets Marcus was standing by, would eventually be sold to those interested in buying high-quality leather at a discounted rate.

It was all profit for Marcus. Everything had been liberated from their delivery trucks at no cost to the Shadow Vipers, so all proceeds from any sales went right into their pockets.

They were criminals, not good Samaritans.

Sue him.

The real hardware—guns, drugs, and other illegal items—were safely locked in his secret room. A room Gavin knew absolutely nothing about... he hoped.

"Here. Which one do you want?" Marcus asked, pointing to the leather jackets hanging on racks.

"What? I can have one?" Gavin asked, seeming shocked by the offer.

"Yeah, and when you're done, I'll take you into the city to buy some clothing. It's not like you packed a bag when you decided to enter the *Viper Protection Program*." Marcus gave him a tiny smirk. He kind of liked the sound of that.

Gavin let out a squeak as he began perusing the designer jackets laid out before him. "Jesus, these are gorgeous." Gavin pulled one out and held it up in front of him. "Wow."

Then he froze.

"Wait. Are all of these... stolen?"

Marcus shrugged. They were going to be sold to someone else eventually. Who cared how these items got in his possession?

Marcus could see the conflict storming in his eyes. He took the jacket from his hands and held it open so Gavin could slip inside.

"Yup, that is definitely the one for you," Marcus whispered, turning the boy so he could check himself out in the mirror. "What do you think?"

The boy was good-looking to begin with. His dark hair against his piercing blue eyes added a sleek contrast that could only be described as... mesmerizing.

Add to that the badass leather jacket Marcus had just thrown onto him. *Oh, Mama.*

Staring at himself in the mirror, Gavin's eyes lit up when he saw his reflection. "Wow."

"Yup. It gives you that badass biker look. Now you look

like you are one of us." Marcus slapped Gavin on the arm. "Now let's go get you some clothes to go with that jacket."

Turning, Marcus headed back upstairs, with Gavin close behind him. They headed out to the back of the bar, where Marcus had his Harley parked.

"Here," Marcus said, passing Gavin a helmet and helping him up onto his bike.

"Hold on tight, and don't let go," Marcus explained, wrapping Gavin's arms around his waist as he started up the bike.

"I've never been on a motorcycle before!" Gavin shouted over the roar of the engine.

"Hang tight!" Marcus warned as he peeled the bike out of the parking lot without warning.

A car honked its horn as Marcus cut past the driver, missing the car by only a few feet. Marcus felt Gavin's grip on him tighten as he buried his face into his back.

Feeling the boy cling to him, knowing he was the only thing that stood between him and certain death, made Marcus feel powerful.

His whole life, Marcus had been a protector, a provider, a brother, a pseudo-father, and for the past ten-plus years, a leader. So many people looked up to him and relied on him to guide them and help keep them safe and out of jail.

Marcus loved it.

He loved that feeling of being needed, being counted on. The knowledge that people depended on him. He might put on a growly demeanor, but secretly, he loved it.

Now, feeling Gavin's face pressed into his body, he felt important. He felt needed.

They drove about twenty minutes north to these really cool clothing stores that Ace and Lucas liked to shop at. He figured that Gavin would have similar tastes and might appreciate getting clothing that actually fit his physical measurements.

Shopping from broken-down trucks did not always provide the wearer with the appropriate measurements they were looking for. One kind of got what was available. And there were no returns or exchanges for sizes.

But Marcus wasn't cheap. He planned on buying Gavin a big enough wardrobe to ensure that he never had to wear the same outfit twice while he was staying with him.

Seeing the vulnerable look on Gavin's face this morning when Marcus found him sleeping outside his bedroom door—too afraid to ask if he could sleep with him in his bed—nearly broke his heart. It reminded him of when Ace used to have nightmares as a young boy, then sneak into his bed to sleep, snuggling into him, needing his protection from the monsters of his dreams.

Ace never ran to either of their parents. He sought Marcus out, knowing his big brother would always be there to have his back and protect him.

Once a protector, always a protector.

Marcus would be whatever it was that Gavin needed. A protector. A provider. A person to listen.

Still clinging for dear life, Marcus could feel Gavin

laughing behind him and having the time of his life. Marcus wasn't wearing his helmet, but he had a Bluetooth in his ear so they could communicate if needed.

The sound of Gavin's laugh warmed Marcus's belly.

8

GAVIN

Riding on the back of Marcus's Harley, Gavin had never felt so alive.

The wind whipping against his face, the rumble of the engine between his legs, and the feel of a big, solid man pressed up against his chest. He instinctively tightened his hold around his protector and smiled.

This moment, right here, almost made the attempted murder date worth it. Almost. But not really. He still preferred living over being unalived by a psychotic serial killer who clearly had intimacy issues.

He might be craving love and romance and a man obsessed with him, but drugging and murder were where he drew the line.

They pulled into a parking spot, and Marcus kicked out his leg before killing the engine.

A few women paused to watch the hunky biker as he

extended his hand to help Gavin off his bike, then stepped off himself.

What a gentleman.

Gavin tried not to gloat as the three thirsty-looking women curled up their noses at the sight of him removing his helmet and passing it back to Marcus to deal with.

Yes, women, he had a big, strong man at his beck and call.

"Holy, that was amazing!" Gavin gushed, slapping Marcus on the shoulder as they walked toward the clothing shop. "Now I understand why bikers say they feel so free riding the open road!"

Marcus pulled off his sunglasses and gave him a smirk. His chestnut eyes seemed to give away the joy he felt every time he sat on his bike.

"I've been riding since I was fifteen. I had a buddy who owned an auto shop, and he and I used to work on old dirt bikes together. One summer, we found an old Harley out at the scrapyard. We spent the summer fixing her up, then the fall learning how to ride without killing ourselves." Marcus breathed in a lungful of oxygen as he glanced up at the sky. "I swear, that summer was when I fell in love with bikes and realized I wanted to be part of the Shadow Vipers."

"So, you joined a biker gang at fifteen?" Gavin asked, glancing over his shoulder as Marcus held the door open for him.

"Well, no. My buddy and I started hanging around with guys we knew were in the gang, being those annoying teenagers who follow or worship guys they want to get in with. Eventually, we wore them down." He gave Gavin a wink.

They spent the next two hours going from shop to shop, buying jeans, shirts, and boots that Gavin thought would look good on him. He even bought a few pairs of underwear he thought were hot as fuck, hoping that eventually he would get a certain dark, growly biker to rip them off him with his teeth.

Lifting his gaze, Gavin caught a glimpse of Marcus trying on a shirt in the changing room mirror. His body was fit, with a light dusting of chest hair. To add to the bad-boy hotness, Marcus had a dark tribal tattoo that extended across his chest and down his left bicep.

Holy fuck. Could the man get any hotter? Gavin just about creamed himself when he got a glimpse of his bare chest.

Knowing that Daddy Marcus was rocking all that man under those tight-fitting shirts was short-circuiting Gavin's brain.

With their bags in hand, they walked back in the direction of Marcus's Harley.

They were almost at the parking lot where they left the bike when a high-pitched squeal left Gavin's body.

Marcus jumped, startled, and looked like he was ready to punch someone in the face.

"Oh my god! They're so cute!" Gavin shouted, dropping his bags and running toward the basket of puppies sitting out under a large tree next to a woman reading a book.

The woman started laughing as Gavin dropped to his knees, and the puppies began climbing over themselves, trying to get to their new best friend.

"I think they like you," the woman said, while Gavin tried his best not to vibrate out of his skin.

"Oh, they are just the cutest things! Can I pick them up?"

"Sure! Take as many as you like. I'm trying to find them new homes."

Gavin's eyes went wide as his body overdosed with joy. His head immediately snapped back, staring up at the dark giant currently blocking the sun.

"Can I? Can we?" Gavin begged, trying his best to look cute as a button. He knew he was well past his cute and innocent phase, but the puppies were depending on his powers of cuteness to win over the heart of the growly, mean ogre.

Annoyed frown lines appeared as Marcus put his stern daddy face back into position.

"Are you nuts? You're not adopting a puppy and taking it back to my house. You can buy your own damn puppy when you leave and go back to wherever it is that you came from," Marcus growled, his eyes locked on Gavin's, clearly ignoring the three adorable puppies he currently had clutched to his chest like furry armor.

But... puppies!

Cute and cuddly puppies!

The woman sitting against the tree looked up at them as if she were witnessing a scene from *Misery* or something.

Gavin opened his mouth to argue, but changed his mind when he realized that Marcus was right. He was just a guest in his home. He was lucky to be staying over at all.

Slowly, he handed the puppies back to the woman.

"Sorry, Daddy's not exactly an animal lover, so it would seem."

The woman gave Marcus a look that showed just how much she hated non-animal lovers.

"It's more like, you don't live with me, so why would you adopt a puppy and mess up the house you are temporarily staying in?" Marcus tried to defend.

Gavin let out a huff and gave his puppy friends one last pat on the head. "Sorry, guys, Daddy doesn't like happiness and rainbows. I'm sure you will find the perfect forever home filled with love and joy and non-growly daddies."

Marcus rolled his eyes, then looked down at the woman. "I just met this kid the other day. I'm not the horrible monster this drama queen is making me out to be."

The woman gave him a stare.

"Look. I even took the twerp shopping. All on me!" Marcus argued, holding up his and Gavin's bags he had abandoned when he spotted the basket filled with four-legged joy and happiness.

"Whatever you say, Mr. Grump," Gavin said, getting up from his knees and giving the puppies one last wave of his fingers.

"Just get your ass back on the bike. I'm too old for this shit," Marcus huffed, turning and walking back toward his ride.

Gavin gave the woman a wink. "He's so much fun to tease."

The woman gave him a smile. "He's not too bad on the eyes either."

9

MARCUS

By the time they got home, Marcus ordered some takeout, which they wolfed down in front of the TV, drinking sodas and beer.

Gavin sat on the floor with his back against the sofa, while Marcus lounged on the couch, shirtless, in just a pair of joggers.

"Pass the spring rolls," Marcus ordered, balancing his plate on his stomach as Gavin passed him the box over his head without looking up from his phone.

Marcus grabbed a roll and then pushed the box back toward the boy.

"What's got your attention all wrapped up?" Marcus asked, biting into the spring roll, then placing the other half down on his plate.

"Huh?" he asked, turning his head slightly in Marcus's direction.

“The phone. What’s so interesting?”

“Oh. Nothing. Just checking how my posts are trending.”

“Trending?” Marcus asked, taking another bite of his spring roll.

It had been Gavin’s idea to order Chinese food. Marcus wasn’t a huge fan, but he was really liking these spring roll thingies.

Gavin turned so his elbow was propped up on the sofa, touching the side of Marcus’s ribs, while he held his phone so Marcus could see.

“See these numbers down here?” Gavin asked, pointing to the numbers listed on each photo. “That is the number of people who viewed my posts. The more people who view, comment, and like my posts, the more engagement I get. The bigger my following, the more money I make from brand partnerships and sponsored content.”

“You make money by posting pictures online?” Marcus asked, his eyebrows scrunching together.

“Well, yes. Kind of. I’m what you would call a social media influencer.”

Marcus couldn’t help but chuckle.

“A social media what?”

“Influencer. Don’t laugh. It’s a real job. Right now, I have one point eight million followers on social media. I’m pulling in a good ten to fifteen thousand dollars a month by being an influencer. It all depends on which products and brands I’m posting about.”

Marcus began to choke on his food.

Sitting up, he placed his plate down on the coffee table and continued coughing until the killer pea cleared his throat.

"You make how much? For doing what exactly?"

"I post reviews of products, restaurants, stores, and tell people what they should or shouldn't wear, and what they should or shouldn't buy. I promote products and places, and I influence people online."

Nodding, Marcus stood up and walked toward the hallway. "I guess that makes me an influencer as well."

Gavin looked up at him. "How do you figure?"

"I tell people what to do, and then they do it." He turned and walked toward the bathroom.

"That's not how it works," Gavin shouted after him, mockingly.

Stepping out of his underwear, Marcus adjusted the water once more before stepping into the shower.

The day had been way too fucking long. What he really needed now was a nice, long, hot shower and a good tug on his meat.

He couldn't remember the last time he busted a nut. Was it three days? Five? Come to think of it, when was the last time he had his dick sucked?

It was the redhead who came into the bar with her

friends about a month ago. She wouldn't stop smiling at him until he stepped out back and unzipped his fly. Her mouth fell open, and Marcus showed her why he was the leader of the Shadow Vipers.

Fuck, that woman knew how to swallow a cock and play with a man's balls.

Had it really been a whole fuckin' month since he had his nuts played with? Damn, his life really sucked.

Building up a nice lather, he ran his hand along the length of his cock and began enjoying the feel of his calloused hands.

"Mmm, take that cock, babe," Marcus growled under his breath thinking about his last experience. He closed his eyes and tilted his head back under the water.

"You know, just because you bark orders at people and scare them into doing what you want does not make you an influencer," Gavin rambled as he walked into the bathroom without even knocking.

Marcus jerked forward, startled. He could see Gavin's outline through the thin shower curtain. He was standing at the sink, putting toothpaste on his brush.

"Umm, what the fuck, dude? I'm in here!" Marcus growled.

"Yeah. So? I've got food stuck in my teeth, and I need to get it out before I lose it."

Marcus placed his hands in front of his junk, hoping he could cover up his rather large predicament.

"So, what's your deal anyway?" Gavin asked, toothbrush in mouth as he began to scrub away. "You got a girlfriend or something? You never really answered my question the other day."

Using one hand to wipe water from his eyes, Marcus tried to will his cock to go down.

"No. No girlfriend."

"Boyfriend?" Gavin asked, his voice rising an octave as he waited expectantly for an answer.

"No boyfriend."

"So you just do random hookups whenever you get horny," Gavin concluded.

"Umm... that's none of your business," Marcus barked back.

He wasn't exactly sure how to answer that question. He didn't like using apps for sex since most of the people never looked like their pictures. He just kind of fucked whenever someone hit on him.

Most were just drunken, last-call fucks, either in the bathroom or out behind the bar. A few had been spur-of-the-moment, outdoor romps when no other place was available.

He didn't exactly do the dating, relationship thing, so bedroom sex wasn't that frequent.

Marcus was the leader of the Shadow Vipers. He fucked wherever and whenever he wanted. He didn't do romance or take people on dates. He had too many obligations and things to worry about to let something like his dick control his life.

No. It was easier to satisfy his urge by getting his dick wet, then move on with his life after his balls were empty.

The rest of the guys were free to run around like horn-dogs loose at a biker party, but he was their leader. He had to make sure that everyone was safe and taken care of.

"Oh, come on. Big, strong guy like you must get laid all the time," Gavin murmured through a mouthful of dental floss.

Marcus could see his silhouette through the curtain and wondered just how much Gavin could see of him.

"I do fine," Marcus answered, picking up the soap and deciding to continue with his shower. He began by soaping his underarms, then moving on to his chest and stomach. He had a nice lather going as he soaped up his body.

Next, he placed his foot on the edge of the tub and began washing his thigh.

Gavin gave a whistle.

"Judging by that hog dangling between your legs, I'm pretty sure it gets lots of attention." Gavin chuckled as Marcus quickly moved to cover his junk.

"Will you get out, you little perve," Marcus barked, feeling his cheeks flush at the comment.

"I'm just saying. If you ever need a mouth to service that hog or an ass to take out all that pent-up aggression on, I'd happily volunteer myself as tribute. No questions asked, no commitment needed." Gavin chuckled as he exited the bathroom. "Night, Daddy!"

Marcus let out an exhausted breath. This kid was going to be the death of him.

It was just after four a.m. when Marcus woke. His mouth was dry, and he needed a glass of water.

Hopping out of bed, Marcus walked toward the hallway, then stopped once he reached his bedroom door.

Sitting up against the wall, with his head fallen forward in a position that could not have been comfortable, was Gavin.

The poor kid was sleeping just outside his bedroom door in the same position he'd found him the previous night. Clearly, he was still having trouble sleeping alone.

Exhaling, Marcus reached down and scooped up the sleeping fireball, gently bouncing him in his arms until he had a proper, firm grip.

Looking between his bedroom and Gavin's at the other end of the hallway, Marcus decided to let Gavin stay in his bed for the night.

His feet padded along the floor quietly as he made his way into his bedroom.

Carefully, Marcus lowered Gavin onto his bed, his black satin sheet crumpling under the weight of the young man's sleeping body.

Yes, Marcus liked the cool feel of smooth satin sheets pressed up against his normally naked body while he was trying to sleep in the warm summer heat. Nothing felt better.

Well... a few things felt better...

Once he had Gavin settled in his bed, he stood there for a moment, wondering what the boy was dreaming about. He looked peaceful... calm and at ease. Gently, he brushed a few stray strands of hair away from his forehead.

Gavin let out a soft moan before rolling over and snuggling into the pillow beneath him, completely unaware of his new location.

They were going to have to come up with some sort of arrangement. Marcus was not going to spend the next, god knows how many nights, sleeping with this little koala bear clinging to his side.

Nope. Sharing his bed was not something that Marcus ever did—except when Ace was younger. But Ace was different. He was his little bro.

This little snoring koala was not so innocent. Marcus was liable to roll over in the middle of the night, only to discover that the little black-haired, blue-eyed demon was busy sucking on his knob.

Marcus tried not to chuckle.

His eyes slid down Gavin's slumbering body and settled on the two perfectly sculpted globes, hidden beneath a thin layer of red fabric. There was something about the way the material fell slightly between Gavin's ass cheeks that made Marcus's lips suddenly very dry.

He licked his lips, wondering what it would feel like to bury his face between the boy's cheeks and devour that tight little hole, which was just begging to be destroyed.

Marcus felt his cock begin to swell.

Fuck. He needed to get laid.

And soon.

Turning, Marcus headed to the kitchen to grab a glass of water and quench the thirst he was suddenly dying from.

10

GAVIN

Sluggishly, Gavin's eyes began to open.

He wasn't sure where exactly he was, but he didn't have an overwhelming sense of panic or danger, so he was pretty sure wherever he was, he was fine and safe.

Slowly, the warm surface beneath him began to rise and fall.

Gavin froze.

He was cuddled up against someone.

His eyes shifted and then quickly fixed on the black ink carved into the chest he had his head resting on.

The body was warm and firm and offered just the right amount of comfort and support that led to one of the best nights' sleep Gavin had ever enjoyed.

Swallowing hard, Gavin's eyes slid farther down, moving across Marcus's chest, and down to his perfectly sculpted abs.

Jesus, the man was in his late thirties yet rocked the bod of a fucking Norse god.

The man was definitely not a stranger to the gym. And judging by those biceps... *my god!*

Licking his lips, Gavin continued his visual exploration of the biker god beneath him.

Gavin's eyes went wide.

Holy. Shit.

Pointing straight up at his face was one of the biggest dicks he had ever seen!

Well, not exactly a dick. But the shape of a dick, safely tucked behind a layer of fabric.

Thank god, because if that dick had been out in the open, staring angrily up at him, he might have had to defend himself by attacking and biting that fucking head off. Okay, perhaps not bite, but swallow. Long and deep. And as sloppily as humanly possible.

Like seriously? What fucking man is allowed to have a fucking dick that big and that thick?

Weren't there rules against this sort of thing?

Like, nobody outside of porn is allowed to carry such a big and lethal weapon.

How were gay boys supposed to go about living their lives, knowing that a monster like that existed? And that it was attached to one of the most growly, sexy, hot dudes he had ever laid eyes on.

No. Seriously. It wasn't fair.

What the hell was in the water in Baton, New Mexico, that allowed a monster like that to grow on a man so sexy?

Swallowing hard, Gavin wasn't sure if he would ever be the same.

Knowing that something like that existed, and on a man he was sharing a house with? And now, sharing a bed with?

Gavin felt his dick begin to grow.

Great. Now his cock wanted in on the action.

No. He was just going to lie here, quiet as a mouse, silently giving worship to the eighth greatest wonder of the world.

Beep!

Gavin and the man beneath him both startled.

Marcus let out a groan as he extended his arm and picked up his cell phone from the bedside table.

Fucking technology.

"Ello?" Marcus whispered, still half asleep and unaware of the worshipper currently attached to his chest.

Gavin lay there, trying not to move or make himself known. He wondered how long he could lie there before the grisly giant beneath him realized that something needy was attached to his body.

It didn't take long.

He felt the body beneath him shift as Marcus lifted his head to see what was clinging to him.

"What? Come again?" Marcus asked, his voice becoming clearer the more awake he became. "Oh, really. He said that?"

Gavin grimaced when a big, meaty paw landed on his shoulder, pulling him away from his warm, comfortable pillow.

Swinging his legs over the bed, Marcus stood, then turned as if looking for something on the floor.

Smiling, Gavin wondered how long it would take for Marcus to realize that the reason he couldn't find whatever it was he was looking for was probably because his massive monster dick boner was most likely blocking his view.

Marcus glanced down, finally noticing the solid rod in his underwear. He adjusted himself, gripping it firmly as he moved it to the side. Then he looked up at Gavin, who was staring at him like a hungry gazelle.

"Seems like we're going to have to teach this punk a lesson," Marcus said into the phone. He bent down and retrieved his jeans before glancing over at Gavin once more. He didn't make any effort at covering up his morning wood. "Tell Nikolai to bring his babies and pick me up in thirty."

He ended the call, then tossed his phone onto the bed.

"Blade and Ace are going to babysit you today at the bar. I have... things to do," Marcus said, carrying his jeans as he headed toward his en suite bathroom.

Gavin let out a breath when he heard the shower start running.

He lay there, staring up at the ceiling, wishing he was in that shower, soaping up every inch of that man's gorgeous body.

Fuck. He needed a good dicking.

"So how are things going?" Ace asked as he passed Gavin a cosmopolitan and took a seat on the other side of the booth.

He took a sip of his chocolate martini, then rolled his eyes as he appeared to have a mouth-gasm.

"God, Alexis makes the most amazing drinks."

Gavin took a sip of his drink and had to agree with his new best friend's assessment.

"So?" Ace asked again, tapping Gavin on the forearm. "How are things going?"

He wasn't really sure what to say. He was just getting to know Ace and didn't exactly want to come across as some pathetic loser who was afraid of his own shadow. But the truth was that he was terrified the Valentine Killer might come after him.

"I don't know. Fine, I guess."

Ace didn't like that answer. He reached across the table and took his hand.

"You know, it's okay to be low-key freaking out. You survived something traumatic, and no one is expecting you to be alright in the head. Trust me, we all have our fair share of trauma and fucked-up stories. Blade's father tried to kill him, Nikolai and his boyfriend were sex trafficked, and I've been battling abandonment issues since I was three." Ace let out a chuckle.

Gavin stared at the drink before him. Ace had a point. Every person had demons they wished they didn't. His just happened to be new.

"Well, to be honest, I'm having trouble sleeping." Ace nodded his head. "Every time I close my eyes, I keep seeing that psycho's face smiling at me."

Ace squeezed his hand. He was just like his brother, caring and compassionate, yet able to stand his ground when needed.

"Thankfully, I have your brother around. Whenever I'm with him, I always feel so safe and protected. It's like I don't need to constantly be looking over my shoulder. I know he won't let anything bad happen to me." Gavin could feel himself smile. Just the thought of Marcus made him feel all warm and tingly.

"That's my big bro for you. Always the protector. Always the caregiver."

"So, what was it like growing up with Marcus? You said he is your stepbrother?"

"Yeah, he's technically my stepbrother, but we don't think of each other like that. We're true brothers in every sense. Our parents were horrible. They preferred drinking and partying, and often forgot that they had kids. It was Marcus who took care of me. He always made sure I had clean clothes for school, ate, and did my homework. He even protected me from bullies who tried to mess with me."

"Guess he's been a protector his whole life."

Ace nodded. "Yeah, I think he loves taking care of people. I know he comes across as all manly and macho, but that's just a role he plays. Deep down, he cares about people and often puts his own needs second."

Placing his martini down on the table, Ace looked around as if to see who might be listening.

"Marcus doesn't know that I know this, but when I was fourteen, I got mono and had to stay indoors for the whole goddamn summer. Marcus spent every day inside, playing video games and watching movies with me. What he didn't tell me was that he turned down a two-week ride across America with a bunch of the guys from the Shadow Vipers. They had been planning the ride for weeks, but when I got sick, he decided not to go. I found out about the trip years later, when Caden let it slip that Marcus had canceled his trip to be there for me. That is the kind of man my brother is."

With each story that Gavin heard, his knight in shining armor became more attractive.

"Yeah, I can see how special your brother really is."

They both continued drinking and sharing stories for the remainder of the afternoon.

11

MARCUS

The air was thick and muggy and clung to Marcus's lungs like a thick layer of honey he just couldn't swallow, no matter how hard he tried.

It was early afternoon, and the sun was bearing down on Marcus and the guys as they sat outside the waste management landfill, watching the New Mexico Greens drink their beers and laugh at their stupid jokes.

The New Mexico Greens was a local street gang that dealt in drugs and petty robbery. They were a smaller crew, just starting out, with maybe nine or ten neighborhoods under their thumb. They were relatively new to Marcus, having done business with them only twice so far.

Amateurs.

Sitting on his bike, Marcus watched the men as he pulled off his riding gloves one by one.

He'd been contemplating what sort of approach he should use this whole ride over.

Should he give Rowan, the leader of the New Mexico Greens, just a warning? Verbally remind him of what happens to people who disrespect and talk shit about him and his crew?

Or should he take more extreme measures and physically show the New Mexico Greens exactly what happens to leaders when they piss off the head of the Shadow Vipers motorcycle gang?

The more he thought about it, the more scenario number two made sense.

He'd shown mercy before, and look how that turned out.

It was twelve years ago when the Shadow Vipers paid a visit to one of the local drug dealers who was behind on three of his payments. Marcus met with the man to discuss the missed payments and what should be done.

The dealer had begged for an extension, saying that his kids were sick and he needed the money to pay for hospital visits, which was why he didn't have the money he owed just yet.

Feeling sorry for the guy, Marcus decided to give the man a two-week extension, while forgiving the interest owed on the outstanding debt.

The dealer was grateful and thanked Marcus profusely.

But that act of kindness was to be rewarded with blood.

Two weeks later, Marcus sent three of his crew members to Colorado to deliver an order of guns a local drug dealer had purchased. That dealer had heard of Marcus's... *compassion* and decided that he really didn't need to pay for all the merchandise he had purchased from Marcus. Instead, he killed two of Marcus's men, then sent the third man home to give a big *fuck you* to the man of compassion.

Realizing in that moment that compassion and mercy did not bode well in the criminal underworld, Marcus decided that business was business, and he would never show mercy or compassion to another man he was doing business with again.

He was the head of the Shadow Vipers and needed to protect his crew. And the best way to do that was through fear and intimidation.

So, option two it was: Show Rowan's crew what happens to leaders when they fuck with the head of the Shadow Vipers.

"So, how do you want to play this?" Caden asked, sitting on his bike next to Nikolai.

Nikolai was loading his gun as he sat there waiting for Marcus's response.

"Want us to go in there first? Clear out the place for you?" Jake asked, pushing his light-brown hair back before spitting into the dirt next to his bike.

"Nah. This is my fight. I say we ride up in there, guns blazing. I'll have a little one-on-one with Rowan, then his crew can watch as I beat the piss out of the little piece of shit. Remind them what happens to assholes who cross the leader of the Shadow Vipers," Marcus explained, smirking as all his men cheered back at him.

No mercy.

"No killing. Just wound the motherfuckers. We want them to be able to spread the word about tonight." Marcus smiled. "Let's ride." Marcus kicked up his sidestand before bringing his bike to life with a monstrous roar.

He floored it, leading his men straight to the landfill's entrance.

A few men started to yell when they spotted Marcus and his crew riding right for them in a cloud of dirt and dust. They didn't have much time or warning before Marcus and his crew crashed through the flimsy fence and began opening fire on all of them.

Men fell to the ground, clutching their knees and gripping their arms. Guns lay scattered around as men dropped them in pain and agony.

Following Marcus's instructions, his men weren't killing them, just incapacitating them, so they were fuckin' useless in defending their leader. The real prize was their leader.

"Hey, hey, boys!" Marcus shouted as he rolled in, firing shots at anything that moved.

Blood splattered everywhere as, one by one, men fell and writhed in pain.

Their entrance was spectacular. A bunch of badass

bikers, rolling in, shooting at any motherfucker who wasn't a Shadow Viper.

Talk about gangster.

Finally, Marcus came to a stop in front of their leader. Pointing his gun at the man, Marcus had to laugh at how fucking dumb he was. He had been sitting in a lounge chair, chugging back beers without so much as a gun within arm's reach.

That was rookie mistake number one. Never be more than a few inches from a gun or weapon. In their line of work, one always needed to be prepared for hell's fire to rain down on them.

Rookie mistake number two? Bad-mouthing criminals who lived within driving distance of where you lived.

"Move another muscle, and I'll blow your fuckin' head off," Marcus growled, shifting his bike into first, then kicking down his sidestand. He turned off his motorcycle, then stepped off the beast, with Nikolai right by his side.

"So, I hear you like talking smack about me and my crew?" Marcus asked, passing Nikolai his gun as he began walking toward the angry man.

Judging by his lack of weapons, the man wasn't much of a threat to Marcus.

Those who'd been smart enough to keep their guns within arm's reach had also been disarmed and were now sitting... or standing, listening to Marcus and his crew bark orders at each of them.

"Not sure what you heard, but I don't appreciate you

assholes rolling up in here and attacking my men. Seems kind of pansy to be shooting at men who aren't even prepared," Rowan growled, his eyes throwing daggers at Marcus as he approached.

Marcus stopped in front of him and knelt so they were face-to-face.

"It's not my fault that your crew is a joke and ill-prepared for an attack. We're criminals, not the UN. You want fair? Go join a tennis league."

Caden and the guys behind him chuckled.

Marcus's jaw tightened as he took in the bratty face of the man who had trash-talked him and his crew. *Fuck this cunt and his motherfuckin' crew.* Marcus grabbed the man by his shirt.

"I hear you've been telling people that I shorted you on our last delivery. That I charged you more than other crews and didn't deliver half the products I said I would."

Rowan's eyes flicked to the men around him. His crew remained silent, either too frightened or unwilling to assist their boss and leader.

"What? I said, nothin' like that," the man spat out.

His body was trembling under Marcus's grip.

He'd seen the signs before—men in power at the mercy of someone much stronger than them. It was hard to take, but even harder to endure when displayed so publicly, especially in front of one's own crew.

It was hard to maintain power when beaten down by another alpha. The pack tended not to follow betas.

It had to be done.

No mercy or compassion.

Marcus had learned that the hard way.

Letting out a growl, Marcus tugged the man up to his feet.

"I'm going to show you what happens to people who disrespect the Shadow Vipers," Marcus snarled.

His jaw tightened, and his mind fell away as he began beating the shit out of the crew leader in front of his own men.

Word would get out of Marcus's cruelty and savagery, once again solidifying his role and position as a man not to be messed with.

The Shadow Vipers were a crew to be respected and feared.

Knuckles bloodied and sore, Marcus finally dropped the battered man into the dirt at his feet. He held out his hand to Niko, who passed him back his gun.

He lifted the gun and pointed it at the man's head.

"Let this be a lesson to you all. This is what happens when you cross the Shadow Vipers. Next time, I'll put a bullet in your head." With that, Marcus released the empty chamber of his gun, causing the beaten man to startle.

Another piece of humiliation thrown at a man who challenged his honor.

He knew he had made an enemy of the man kneeling before him, humiliated. But that was their life.

Criminals didn't get into their line of work to be loved and make friends. They did it for power and money.

And Marcus had both.

Fear came at a cost. Marcus needed to do what was necessary to keep his men safe and ensure the success of his crew and family.

"Let's go, boys," Marcus called, throwing his leg back over his Harley.

They had a long ride home, and he wanted to make a quick stop along the way.

12

GAVIN

"Honey, I'm home!" Gavin called as he entered the house and closed the front door behind him. He walked into the living room and found Marcus sitting on the sofa, flipping through the channels on the television.

"One of these days, that smart mouth of yours is going to get you into trouble," Marcus said, tossing the remote onto the coffee table, then picking up his beer and taking a swig.

"It depends on what you mean by trouble. It's been very naughty since I turned eighteen, but I can't say that anyone has ever complained when it comes to my mouth," Gavin answered, dropping down onto the sofa next to Marcus.

Marcus was once again sitting, shirtless, in nothing but

his joggers. Gavin was quickly discovering that this was Marcus's lounging-around-the-house wear.

"Did everything work out today?" Gavin asked, grabbing Marcus's beer and taking a sip.

Then he spotted Marcus's knuckles.

"Holy shit! Are you okay?" Gavin asked, placing the bottle down on the table and reaching for Marcus's battered hands.

His knuckles were all cut and already scabbing over, clear signs that he had been in a fight earlier in the day. Gavin turned Marcus's big hands over in his, examining both sides, looking for more injuries.

"What happened?" he asked, looking up and seeing the scratches on Marcus's cheek as well. He reached out and softly traced the cuts with his thumb.

Marcus grunted, then pulled his face away from Gavin's fingers.

What the hell had happened to him?

"I'm fine. Just had to take care of some business."

Turning his attention back to Marcus's hands—which still hadn't been pulled away—Gavin ran his fingers over the injuries and grimaced at the pain he must be in.

Typical, hypermacho man, trying to put on a tough face.

While Gavin found the thought of a guy getting into a fight kind of hot, seeing the results of that brawl now made him feel nothing but worry and concern.

"Are you sure? Did you even clean these cuts?" Gavin

asked, suddenly standing and wondering where the man kept his first aid kit.

Marcus let out a chuckle.

"I'm the leader of a motorcycle gang. I don't need my knuckles cleaned every time I get into a scrap."

Gavin looked down at the scruffy man lounging on the sofa as if this were no big deal and nothing to worry about.

What world did this man live in?

When you got into fights, you washed out your wounds, then spent the rest of the night being pampered and waited on.

That was just the way that things were supposed to go.

Marcus was just sitting there, as if nothing had happened.

Shaking his head, Gavin was at a loss for words.

"Don't be stupid. Where's your first aid kit?"

Marcus chuckled. "First aid kit. As if."

Scoffing, Gavin hopped off the sofa and headed to the common bathroom. He searched through the medicine cabinet until he found some hydrogen peroxide. He grabbed the bottle and some paper towels from the kitchen before returning to where the big macho man was resting on the couch, smirking.

Jumping into Nurse Gavin mode, he quickly dabbed some fluid onto the paper towel, then gently pressed it over the man's wounds.

There was a slight hiss from his patient, as the big, bad biker tried to ignore the sting of the peroxide against the open wound.

The cuts mainly looked clean, so Gavin guessed that Marcus probably washed his hands when he first got home. That was good. Hopefully, the peroxide would kill any lingering bacteria that might be present. He wasn't a nurse, so he wasn't exactly sure how to handle a cut or wound, but this was what people did on television all the time.

Plus, he kind of liked taking care of the big lug. Seeing the tough guy fight his hardest to not move a muscle was just the cherry on top.

Their eyes locked together, and for the first time, Gavin swore he saw what looked like appreciation in Marcus's gaze.

Hadn't anyone ever taken care of him before? His mother must have cleaned up his scraped knees and twisted ankles when he was a young hellion running around with his friends.

Gavin didn't know much about Marcus's past, but he felt all warm and tingly staring back into his eyes.

Placing the cap back on the bottle, Gavin quickly tidied up his workspace.

"So? How was your day?" Marcus asked, raising an eyebrow at him.

Shrugging his shoulders, Gavin flopped back down, sitting on one of his legs.

"It was fine, I guess. Played pool with Ace, listened to Damian go on about his three-day trip to Vegas, where he discovered the joys of getting pegged. Apparently,

Nikolai turned him on to it? Are they a couple or something?"

Marcus chuckled.

"No. Nikolai is the badass Russian who works security at the bar. He's engaged to his long-time love, Reid. Nikolai is just... *sexually* adventurous, let's say."

That made sense. Gavin got the feeling that being a member of the Shadow Vipers opened the door to a pretty adventurous sex life.

Was Marcus the same way? Did he normally spend his nights and weekends balls deep in some floozy or whore?

Suddenly, Gavin wanted to murder every last one of Marcus's sexual conquests.

What was he doing? He barely knew the man and was already getting jealous of the man's sexual past? Grow up.

Looking back up at Marcus, he continued.

"Tried to get embarrassing stories about you out of Blade, but the man is surprisingly loyal to you. If he weren't married to your bro, I would have thought he had a hard-on for you."

"Did you ask him about the time I beat his face in when I found out he and my brother were screwing? Tossed him out of his motel room in his underwear. Even then, the guy didn't fight back."

"Yeah, it's a nice little cult you got going on at that bar of yours." Gavin chuckled, leaning back into the plush sofa while he tried not to mentally undress Marcus with his mind.

"You hungry? I can barbecue us up some steaks," Marcus offered.

Gavin gave him an unimpressed look.

"Oh yeah. You're not a carnivore." Gavin nodded in agreement. "Fine, I'll fire up a steak for me and grill some nice carrots and zucchini for you." Marcus stood and hiked up his joggers, which were slung low on his hips.

He made his way around the sofa before he leaned down just inches from Gavin's face and whispered, "Go check inside your room."

Gavin turned and looked up at him, confused and a tad suspicious. *What was the man going on about?*

Slowly, he got up from the sofa and walked down the hallway toward his room. Once he reached the door, he turned the knob and slowly peeked inside.

Sitting in the center of his bed was a brown wicker basket.

What the fuck?

Gavin stepped into the room and made his way over to the bed.

And then, his heart stopped.

Swaddled in a dark-blue fuzzy blanket was the cutest little black-and-white border collie he had ever seen. The puppy's eyes slowly opened, and his nose began to twitch as he sniffed the air around him.

Gavin let out a squeal, then carefully reached into the basket and pulled out the puppy and the blanket at the same time.

"Oh my god! You are so cute!" Gavin squealed, hugging and squishing the little creature into himself.

Rushing from the bedroom, Gavin quickly ran into the kitchen, where Marcus was seasoning a steak at the counter, and slapped a kiss on his cheek.

"Whoa!" Marcus chuckled, appearing caught off guard by the sudden gesture.

"Thank you! Thank you! Thank you!" Gavin screeched, jumping up and down next to the sweetest man he had ever met. "He is just so adorable! And I love him!"

Smiling, Marcus turned toward him, his cheeks a slight shade of pink. "Well, I'm glad you like him. 'Cause he's yours now. So you need to feed him, walk him, train him, and make sure he doesn't piss all over my house."

Gavin nodded, barely hearing a word he said. The four-legged little dude was just too cute to handle.

Then a thought occurred to Gavin, and he froze.

"Wait. You didn't beat up and steal this puppy from that lady by the tree, did you?"

Marcus's mouth dropped open. He appeared shocked and offended by the question at the same time.

"No, of course not. But I'm pretty sure that the blood on my knuckles may have been the reason why the woman practically gave me the puppy for free."

Gavin hugged the puppy close as the little guy licked at his nose and whimpered.

Okay, so the story seemed to check out. He could live with that, even if the woman did give him a discounted puppy out of fear of the crazy man with bloodstains on his hands.

"I love you so much, little guy." The puppy was causing major endorphin overload, and Gavin was finding it hard to concentrate. Then another question occurred to him.

"But... why did you buy me a puppy?" he asked, still confused and overjoyed by the gesture.

"'Cause you seemed like you could use a bit of comfort. Perhaps this little guy will help you through some of the trauma you've faced these past few days."

Marcus was looking at him with what one could only assume was concern when it came to tough biker dudes.

He placed his hand on Gavin's cheek and locked eyes with him once more.

"You know I won't let anything happen to you while you're under my protection, right? The sheriff is going to find that motherfucker, and if he can't, me and the guys will hunt him down ourselves."

Marcus's gaze was so intense that Gavin had no doubt in his mind that Marcus would keep his promise.

He nodded as he tightened his grip on his new puppy. The little furball was actually helping him feel better.

"I know you don't know me, and don't have any reason to trust me just yet, but I hope that in time, you'll feel safe here, behind these doors, and trust that I will never let anything bad happen to you."

But Gavin already had that feeling. That was one of the reasons he had been falling asleep behind Marcus's bedroom door these past few nights. Being close to Marcus made him feel safe and protected. Knowing that his big, growly protector was just steps away calmed his nerves enough for him to relax and let his guard down, eventually giving in to the pull of sleep.

Now he had his own little guard dog to protect him and help him feel safe.

He smiled up at Marcus. Who would have guessed that under all that muscle and rough exterior lived a sweet man with a generous heart?

"Now, can you please move so I can grill up our supper?" Marcus growled, covering up the steaks with some foil before reaching for the pile of vegetables laid out on the counter.

Smiling, Gavin turned and walked into the living room to begin some much-needed puppy time.

He still couldn't believe that the big, growly biker man had bought him a puppy! His very own furry, four-legged bundle of love.

Glancing over his shoulder, he felt his heart expand as he watched the six-foot-four beast of a man chop veggies as he prepared dinner for both him and Gavin.

13

MARCUS

All through dinner, Marcus watched Gavin fawn over the dog. He held the mutt on his lap, trying to feed him scraps from the table—not leftover veggies that Gavin was eating, but bits and pieces of cow flesh that kept magically disappearing off Marcus's plate.

It appeared that their four-legged friend did not follow in *Daddy's* footsteps, but instead preferred to follow in "Big Daddy's" steps, as Gavin so eloquently put it.

Marcus liked the "big" part, but he wasn't sure how he felt about the "Daddy" reference. For some reason, he felt that made him seem old and irrelevant.

He was only thirty-nine, healthy as an ox, and built like a beast. He wouldn't say that he was smoking hot, but women seemed to fall all over themselves trying to get him to take them out back. Whether it was because they wanted to get fucked by the leader of the Shadow

Vipers, or because they just couldn't stand his smoldering good looks, Marcus liked to believe it was because of the latter.

After washing the dishes and watching a few episodes of mindless TV, Marcus excused himself for the night and left Gavin sitting on the floor, playing with his new buddy.

Back in his bedroom, he closed the door behind him—something he hadn't done since the night Gavin moved in—and stripped down to his underwear.

"Ahh, that's much better." Marcus moaned as he lay on his bed, spreading his arms and legs wide, enjoying the coolness of his satin sheets against his warm, mostly naked body.

It didn't take him long to drift off to sleep, only to be woken up by a gentle knock at his door.

The knock was so quiet that at first, he thought he had imagined it.

Hearing the knock again, he opened his eyes and looked at the clock on his nightstand.

It was just after midnight.

Somehow, he had managed to get at least an hour's sleep.

"Marcus?" Gavin's voice called ever so quietly from behind his door.

At least the boy was knocking. He half expected him to barge right in and make himself at home.

"Yeah?" Marcus asked, counting down the seconds until... yup, right on schedule.

The door slowly opened, letting in the soft light from the living room.

"What is it, Gavin?" Marcus asked, turning his head toward the door.

Gavin stood in the doorway, holding his new friend in nothing but his underwear.

"So, I was trying to sleep, but this little guy keeps whining. I think he misses his big daddy."

Marcus tried not to laugh. The excuses this kid was coming up with.

"Oh, is that so?"

"Yup. I told him that you needed your beauty rest and that a man of a certain age needed to go to bed early so his brittle bones and muscles could rest, but *puppy* here refuses to listen. He says that he misses his daddy and wants to cuddle with him... just for a bit." Gavin held up the little runt, who whined and looked at him with sad puppy eyes that strangely matched the ones that *little daddy* was giving him as well.

Like daddy, like son.

"Just for a bit?" Marcus asked, like he actually believed the kid.

"Yup. Ten, fifteen minutes tops."

"And then, puppy will go back to his room?"

Gavin nodded enthusiastically.

"That includes puppy's daddy, as well?"

This time, Gavin just stared at him. He played with his fingers as he cradled the pup in his arms.

Letting out a huff, Marcus tossed open the sheet next to him and waited for Gavin to slide in.

"But the puppy stays on top of the covers. I don't want dog smell rubbing up against my junk and stuff," Marcus growled, watching as Gavin slid in next to him and dropped the puppy on the outer side of the bed.

Gavin slid his back up against Marcus's side and turned to face his puppy, who was quickly snuggling into the warm sheet around him.

Rolling his eyes, Marcus turned onto his side so he was facing Gavin's back and wrapped his arm around Gavin's naked body.

Marcus had hoped that getting Gavin a puppy might help him sleep better at night, but it appeared that the little furball hadn't worked his magic yet.

Fine. One more night in his bed wouldn't hurt, and perhaps it might help Gavin to relax and learn to trust him a bit more.

Pulling Gavin into his body, Marcus laid his head down next to the boy and breathed in the smell of his shampoo. It was the same lavender scent that Marcus had on his head—which made sense considering it was his shampoo in the shower.

A satisfied exhale came from the boy lying next to him as he placed his hand over Marcus's and pulled it tighter against his chest.

Okay, fine. This was probably not what Sheriff Burke had in mind when he said to watch over his witness, but it was what was best for the boy in the end.

People often overlook the psychological impact of trauma—the memories and nightmares they endure, especially when alone late at night. If Marcus could help reduce that pain in any way, he was damn well going to.

Closing his eyes, he let the sound of Gavin's soft breathing lull him off to sleep.

Cold wetness on his face pulled Marcus from a wonderful dream he was having in which he was riding down the I-90, shooting bullets at Blade as he ran alongside the road in nothing but his boxers and bunny ears.

Hearing the man yelp every time a bullet hit his feet, and watching him jump, brought a warm, fuzzy feeling to the pit of his stomach and a huge smile to the front of his face. There was nothing more satisfying than dreaming he was humiliating that dumbass fuck-twad who had defiled his little brother. Husband or not, it was his dream, and he could do whatever he wanted to that cunt of a man.

Another swipe of wetness across his cheek, followed by a soft chuckle beside him, had Marcus slowly opening one eye.

If Gavin was licking his face, the boy was a dead man.

Bright blue eyes set against a head of jet-black hair beamed down at him as an excited puppy practically attacked his face.

Marcus jumped back.

"What the fuck?" he growled.

Gavin let go of the hyperactive puppy, who immediately dropped onto Marcus's face and began rubbing its ass all over Marcus's mouth and cheek as it searched for dry surfaces it had not yet licked.

Marcus grabbed the puppy with one giant paw and lifted the whimpering creature off his face.

He tossed the puppy at Gavin, who immediately caught his baby with a terrified gasp.

"Next time that thing sits on my face, I'm locking it outside with a mama eagle."

Gavin's mouth dropped open in horror.

"But—you wouldn't! Not to our baby!" He clutched the whiny puppy to his chest, who was still making every attempt possible to leap out of Gavin's arms and lick-attack Marcus's face.

Stubborn dog.

Marcus gave Gavin a look.

"Please tell me you're not one of those people."

"What people?" Gavin asked, caressing his baby while holding him protectively against his chest.

"Those, 'my pet is my baby' freaks." Marcus couldn't stand those people who walked around acting like a four-legged creature that licks its own balls and humps every surface in their home was an actual human being.

No, he wasn't coming to Pongo's birthday, and he didn't care whether your goldfish had anxiety. As far as he was concerned, living with someone like that was permission to commit murder.

"Wow, someone is a grumpy-puss when they first wake up in the morning," Gavin muttered, turning his attention back to his baby.

"Just when I wake up to something wet licking my face."

"What about waking up to something wet licking you somewhere else?" Gavin asked in one of his flirty tones.

He walked right into that one.

He turned and gave Gavin a face.

Speaking of which, he reached for the sheet and pulled it up over his morning wood.

"Don't worry. I barely peeked."

"Sure you didn't."

"Well, well, what is this?" a voice asked from their bedroom doorway, startling both Marcus and Gavin.

Their guard dog/hyperactive ADHD furball lunged from Gavin's arms and dove toward the two men standing in Marcus's doorway.

Glad to see that the little pup has a keen sense of survival skills, leaping over the edge of the bed in an attempt to share more doggy-breath kisses—he assumed, of course.

Ace barely caught the flying pup in his arms before he, too, got attacked by love and kisses.

"I don't know what's more shocking, finding out the boss is boning the new kid? Or knowing that big, bad Daddy sleeps with a puppy in bed?" Blade mocked, smirking at Marcus before turning to the excited furball to show it some love.

"Ace, pass me my gun. I need to shoot your husband in the face," Marcus deadpanned, resting his head against his pillow once again.

"Always with the violence," Blade responded without even looking in Marcus's direction.

"So, who's this little guy?" Ace asked, dropping down on the bed between Marcus and Gavin's feet.

"I still haven't thought of a name yet. But Marcus surprised me with him last night," Gavin gushed, moving closer so he could pet his baby as well.

"Oh, isn't that sweet of him?" Blade mocked, getting dangerously close to catching a bullet with his teeth.

"That's me, all sweet and cuddly," Marcus growled.

"Well, you are nice and cuddly," Gavin responded, "Sweet? Only when you're not being licked first thing in the morning."

Ace and Blade looked over at Marcus.

Fuckin' kid.

"He was talking about the dog," Marcus corrected.

"Sure," Ace teased, turning his attention back to the dog.

Letting out a breath, Marcus looked over at the time. "Remind me again why you assholes broke into my house?"

"We came to have breakfast with you. We knocked, but nobody answered," Ace explained.

"So, you decided to walk in," Marcus concluded.

"Yup. We didn't think that you'd be in here, balls deep in the kid you're supposed to be protecting," Blade noted. "Well, I guess it is hard to get to someone when Marcus's big-ass body is wrapped around their target. Smart thinking, boss."

A growl escaped Marcus's lips.

"Perhaps we should go get breakfast started," Ace offered, standing and walking out of the room with the puppy in his hands.

"I'll give you two a few minutes to... finish up in here," Blade offered, backing out of the bedroom and closing the door behind him. "Say, twenty minutes?"

Marcus tossed the bottle of lotion at his bedroom door.

Blade chuckled as he walked down the hallway.

"Well, we do have a bit of time before breakfast is ready?" Gavin offered, reaching under the sheet and grabbing Marcus's quickly thickening cock.

Marcus let out another growl before throwing the sheet off his body.

"Get dressed. We're not boning."

14

MARCUS

After spending the morning listening to Blade and Ace make wiseass jokes about him and Gavin sleeping together and secretly hooking up, Marcus finally walked into Ride 'em Hard a little crabbier than usual.

"Is it just me, or is the big guy a little moodier than usual?" Caden asked Nikolai, assuming that Marcus couldn't hear him.

Marcus growled as he looked over the balance sheets and books he had laid out on the large table at the back of the bar.

It was too quiet in his office to work, so he set up shop in the back of the bar, where they usually prepared food and snacks for paying customers. It was early afternoon, so the only ones drinking were the usual drunks and retirees who had nothing better to do.

"Oh, the boss is just pissed that we caught him cuddling with his little twinkie this morning. It was cute. They were playing with their little puppy and everything. Very Hallmark Christmas special-ly," Blade explained, only adding to Marcus's sour mood.

Seriously, sometimes he wondered why he kept the guy around.

Because he is loyal and big-hearted, and even though he is sticking it to your little bro, deep down, you know you love the prick, Marcus heard that pesky voice inside his head say.

"We weren't cuddling," Marcus clarified, refusing to look up from his books and give the story any more credence than was necessary.

"You were both in your underwear, the boy was nestled into your chest, and you were both playing with the mutt. Sounds like cuddling to me," Blade noted. Then he turned to Caden and Nikolai. "Oh, and the dude had a massive boner."

"Who? Gavin?" Caden asked, his eyes suddenly widening.

"No. The boss!" Blade clarified, nodding his head toward him.

"I didn't have a boner," Marcus growled, this time looking up and glaring at his men.

"Okay, it was covered by a sheet, but still, I've never seen a sheet so high. It might even rival yours, you freaky Russian," Blade added, turning to his buddy.

Before Blade got serious with Ace, he and Nikolai used

to fuck chicks together all the time. It was kind of their... thing.

It was a well-known fact within the Shadow Vipers that Nikolai's cock was... well, let's just say, way above average. The running joke was that when God made Nikolai's cock, he used double the clay.

Marcus and Nikolai had never actually compared cock sizes, but based on his visual assessment, he was pretty sure that the Russian had him beat. Perhaps by only an inch.

"When you're done idolizing my cock, can we get down to business?" Marcus asked, slamming closed one of the books he had been reviewing.

"Yeah, sure, boss," the guys mumbled as they gathered around the table he was sitting at.

"Has there been any word from our friend on the West Coast?" Marcus asked, looking up at Caden.

"Yeah. They've been busy moving shipments, and everything seems back on track, with delivery scheduled for mid-next week."

"Good. Hopefully, that asshole learned his lesson and doesn't need another reminder of who he's dealing with." Every so often, some young punk would get it into his head that he didn't need to follow orders and could do whatever the fuck he wanted. Whenever that happened, Marcus would just send a few of his guys to pay them a visit and remind them of their role and who was really in charge.

"And, what about this thing with the sheriff?" Nikolai asked.

"What thing?" Marcus asked, his eyes shifting to the blond-haired Russian.

"Do we sit back and let Burke catch this killer? Or do we take matters into our own hands and hunt him down ourselves?"

Marcus looked around the room at his boys. Every one of them would be willing to hunt down this man if he asked them to. But now wasn't the time.

"For now, we give Burke and his team a chance to bring in this motherfucker on their own. Right now, Gavin is safe, and there is no immediate danger to the public. Burke thinks the Valentine Killer ran off, knowing that someone actually saw his face. He doesn't think the killer will try anything else, at least not for the immediate future. If the cops can't locate him in the next few weeks..." Marcus paused, considering his words once more. "Then we can take matters into our own hands and hunt down this pathetic monster."

The guys nodded, all seeming in support of this plan.

"So, in the meantime, you're going to continue to service... I mean, *protect* this guy," Blade noted with a mischievous smirk on his face.

"There's nothing going on between Gavin and me," Marcus argued, a little louder than he originally intended. "I'm not even gay."

"Hey, don't knock it until you try it," Niko chimed in.

Nikolai had been straight until his old best friend, whom he thought was dead, suddenly reappeared in his life. Ever since then, Nikolai has been overindulging in the wonderful world of dude-sex.

Seriously, he was like an addict who had been released from his leash.

Marcus shook his head. "I'm not saying that there's anything wrong with fucking a guy... I'm just saying that I've only ever buried my dick in pussy."

"Well, that dude sure wants your dick," Blade added, hopping up on the table and sitting his ass next to Marcus's books. "And I've got to say, when it comes to tight little peaches, that boy's got one set of cheeks you might want to clap."

"You're married to my brother," Marcus growled.

Blade's eyes went wide, and his arms shot out in front of him. "Hey! I didn't mean for me. I'm just saying that if you were to explore the magical world of man-on-man sex, that dude is ready and willing and probably has the experience to make your toes curl."

Listening to the way Blade was talking about Gavin really began to irk him. The man had no respect. Just because Gavin was cute and flirty, and smelled like sin and debauchery every time he was near him, did not mean the boy had slept with every single man who pulled out his dick.

How many men had Gavin been with? How many loads had he swallowed before he hopped into bed with him?

What did it matter? It wasn't like he was a saint himself. He'd eaten and fucked more pussy than half the men in this town. Being the leader of the Shadow Vipers was like having a revolving door of sexual partners available at his beck and call.

"When was the last time you got laid?" Nikolai asked.

"When was the last time you went out on a date?" Caden added.

Marcus looked around the room at the guys he now considered family. He was the father, and these mouthy little bitches were his kids. Even the beefy Russian, who was almost the same age as him, he still considered under his supervision. Someone had to make sure these idiots didn't die or get arrested.

Shaking his head, Marcus opened one of the books in front of him. "I don't have time for dating and relationships. When I'm horny, I go out and get my dick sucked. End of story."

"That's the stupidest load of shit I've ever heard," Blade responded. "What do you mean you don't have time?"

Marcus's gaze narrowed as he locked eyes with his brother-in-law. The man could be so infuriating at times.

"I'm the boss. The head of this crew. My job is to make all the decisions, keep you all safe and out of harm's way, and make sure you all stay out of jail. I can't afford to be distracted by lovers and whiny partners who complain that I don't text them all the time, or that I promised to be home in time for dinner. Or who gets mad at me because I forgot it was our anniversary. No, my focus is and always will be on the safety and success of this family."

Marcus slammed the book in front of him closed, then stood up and walked into the bar. He needed a fucking drink.

Inside the bar, he waited for Alexis to bring him a shot of whiskey and a beer.

"Look, boss," Nikolai said, sliding in next to Marcus. "I hear what you are saying, and we all love you for that. But what kind of life are you living without any love or someone special to share it with?"

Marcus picked up the shot of whiskey and threw it back before reaching for the bottle of beer.

"I know what you're saying, Niko. But a man in my position can't just focus on what he wants. I need to always consider the effect my actions will have on the rest of the crew and this entire family. What if the person I fall in love with doesn't agree with this lifestyle? What if that person says something they shouldn't and then puts this family at risk? What if I'm so distracted by the cheesy love I feel that I miss something important and end up getting myself or someone else I love killed?" Marcus looked over at Niko, who was looking back at him with sympathetic eyes. "Unlike you guys, I can't afford to be selfish. I'm not free to love who I want. I'm not free to give myself to someone else. There will always be a part of me that I cannot share with that person. It's just the way things are."

Nikolai placed his hand on Marcus's shoulder and gave

him a squeeze. He understood what the guys were saying and where they were coming from, but it was just easier and safer for them all if he just kept things casual and just hooked up whenever he got horny.

Relationships weren't meant for everyone.

15

GAVIN

Staring at the image, Gavin clicked the edit button, then adjusted the color and zoomed in on the costume gloves and hat that sat on the table.

There. That was perfect.

Gavin believed that one should always do what they could to enhance every shot and put forth the best image possible. There was beauty in photos, but taking the time to enhance that beauty just showed the world how much you really cared.

It was a mantra he had lived by ever since deciding to focus on enhancing his brand and public image.

If one wanted to be a top-notch influencer, they needed to create a brand, spend years harnessing that brand, and build a following that supported that brand.

Gavin's brand was urban gay boy meets top-shelf life. He posted images of clubs and restaurants that he and his fellow influencers often frequented. He had spent years building a network of "friends" with whom he often attended openings, tried out new and trendy restaurants, and even celebrated birthdays. The events were always staged and superficial. It was all for the cameras, and they all barely spoke with one another. If they did speak, it was to suggest certain photos or complain about someone's outfit.

Gavin and his friends didn't have a conventional friendship—one based on actually liking the person and wanting to spend time with them. Their friendship consisted of helping each other create an illusion of a fabulous life that everyone was addicted to viewing.

There was a particular high one got from being loved, and it only got amplified the longer they relied on social media to justify their self-worth.

It wasn't healthy, but Gavin wasn't under any delusion that his need to be praised by his followers stemmed from the neglect by his parents.

Gavin was twelve years old when he entered the science fair, hoping to gain his parents' praise if he could only win first prize.

He had spent two weeks researching topics and speaking with fellow classmates until he finally decided to build a model train that could run on the power of citrus fruit.

He spent weeks designing the experiment. Testing and retesting, making adjustments to gather enough acidic power to hopefully run a model train on a continuous loop around his track—a track that he designed himself, adding that personal extra touch he hoped that the judges, as well as his parents, would see and take note of.

The day finally came for the big science fair competition. Gavin had confirmed with his parents three times that morning that they would both be in attendance. Even his nanny, Lilly, had promised to be there to watch and support him.

He was so excited.

When it came his turn to present his project to the judges, he glanced around the gymnasium, but could not spot his mom or his dad.

Finally, he spotted Lilly, who gave him a huge smile and waved like he was the only one in the world!

Gavin was so excited. If Lilly was there, his parents must be buried in the crowd as well.

Taking a breath to calm his nerves, Gavin placed the electrodes into the oranges and watched as his model trains slowly came to life.

The faces of the judges lit up as Gavin's trains circled the track three times before slowing to a stop.

As claps filled the air, the judges passed Gavin the first-place ribbon.

Gavin couldn't believe it! First place!

His head snapped around the room, looking for his parents. They were going to be so proud of him.

The more he searched, the more the excitement he felt in his stomach began to die.

Lilly finally approached, smiling ear to ear. She gave him a hug and told him how proud she was of him.

"Thanks, Lilly. But where's Mom and Dad?"

The look in his nanny's eyes confirmed his suspicions. His parents hadn't come once again.

"They both had last-minute conference calls come up, love. They wished they could be here, but unfortunately, they couldn't."

Gavin traced the first-place lettering on the ribbon he had been awarded. Once again, he didn't matter to his parents. No matter how much he tried and how hard he worked, he never seemed to be able to catch his parents' attention.

He thought the science fair might be something that would impress his parents, but once again, their jobs took precedence.

So Gavin turned to social media. It was an artificial way for him to get the approval and praise he could never get from his parents.

Over time, he realized that social media could be used for other things as well like making money and spreading the word.

He'd begun working with sponsors and tagging brands and causes that he wanted to bring attention to. Over time, his methods began to pay off. People trusted his opinions and enjoyed being a part of the community he was building.

Eighty percent of his content was still brand-related, but every now and then, he liked to throw in bits and pieces of his actual personal life. Like today, as an example.

"Wow, that photo looks really good!" Ace gushed, looking over Gavin's shoulder as he struggled to see the photo Gavin was editing.

"Thanks. I'm going to add it to a collection of photos highlighting the play and where people can grab tickets."

Ace's head snapped in his direction. "What? You would really do that?"

They were sitting in the park across from the civic center, waiting for Lucas to finish helping the last of the theater kids he was working with on one of their scenes.

Lucas had given them both a sneak preview of the play his theater class was putting on in a few weeks and had happened to mention to Gavin that ticket sales were not where he would have liked them to be. He had created a website and printed out fliers, but he was having difficulty getting the word out. Lucas had mentioned that the money raised from ticket sales would help fund the program the following year, so he was hoping to make as much as possible.

So Gavin thought he would snap a few photos, stitch them into an album, then drop a post on his social media platforms.

Lucas and Ace had been so good to him; he figured this might be a nice way to thank them for everything they had done for him.

"It's really not a big deal. I'm just going to post a few photos highlighting the children's production, with a link to the play's website. Hopefully, that might drive a few sales and help spread the word. Plus, I haven't been on my socials in a few days, and I'm sure my followers are starting to worry."

"What do you mean, worry?" Ace asked, picking up the puppy they still hadn't named and plopping him down in his lap.

"Well, social media influencers always post at least two to five times a day. I haven't posted anything since this whole thing with the Valentine Killer. People are probably wondering where I've disappeared to. If I don't post stuff soon, my followers are going to drop me."

Ace shook his head. "Wow, that sounds intense. And a pain in the ass."

Gavin chuckled. "Don't say anything to Lucas about this. I don't want him to think that I didn't have faith in him pulling this off. I just wanted to do something nice to help spread the word."

"Sure thing," Ace promised.

"Sorry about that," Lucas said, dropping down onto the grass with them and reaching over to pet the puppy. "Now that the kids are all picked up, my attention is all yours!"

"It's pretty amazing what you've done with this program," Gavin complimented, playing with his toes as he enjoyed the warmth from the sun.

Lucas had been asked by the director of social planning to put together a children's theater program from scratch and then help run it.

"Yeah, I just love singing and dancing, and introducing a whole new generation to musical theater."

Seeing Lucas's eyes brighten as he discussed the program touched Gavin deeply. He envied that kind of passion, wishing he could feel that way about something in his own life. Up to now, everything—his life and his job —felt empty and insignificant. Who really cares about the trendiest restaurant or the jeans that make your butt look bigger? They're all just surface-level concerns. When you look closely, none of it truly matters.

What Lucas was doing, teaching kids to sing and dance and to express themselves through movement, was a valuable skill they would carry with them for the rest of their lives. Lucas's impact would stay with them forever.

Now that meant something.

"So, how are things going with you and Marcus? I heard you guys have been sleeping together," Lucas asked, glancing between him and the puppy.

Gavin deadpanned to Ace.

"We're not sleeping together. Well, yes, technically we are sleeping in the same bed, but we're not having sex or anything."

Lucas lowered his head and stared at him from the top of his eyes. It reminded Gavin of how his mother used to look at him whenever she knew he was lying.

"No. I'm serious. Trust me, I'd ride that man till kingdom come if he'd let me, but I swear, he has a will of steel."

Ace chuckled. "Yeah, my big bro is very set in his ways. He can be stubborn as shit, but the key is you need to wear him down. Keep hitting on him and teasing him with that sweet little ass of yours. Eventually, you'll break him down."

"But I thought Marcus was straight?" Lucas asked, stealing the puppy from Ace and snuggling the furball into his chest.

"To be honest, I'm not really sure what my brother's preference is. I've seen him hook up with loads of chicks, but sometimes I get this vibe that maybe he isn't as straight as he seems," Ace explained. "Like two months ago, we were all at the gym, and some little twink started changing in front of him in the locker room. I swear, I saw him get a chub in his joggers."

Hmm, perhaps Mr. Big Tough Guy wasn't so straight after all.

Sexuality was a sliding scale with varying degrees of sexual desire. Some people sat at the ends—being either one hundred percent gay or one hundred percent straight, while others fell somewhere in between—some being more attracted to one sex than the other, while some enjoyed both sexes equally.

Gavin didn't believe that people had to choose where they sat on the spectrum. People's tastes and preferences could evolve over time.

While Marcus might have been hardcore straight when

he was younger, perhaps his dick was starting to lean to the left a tiny bit more with age.

"Well, whatever your brother's preference is, one thing is certain: He is sexy as fuck," Gavin declared.

Ace shook his head.

Gavin didn't care what Ace thought. If Marcus was even five percent gay or questioning, that was five percent of the man's dick that was going to end up in his mouth or ass.

16

MARCUS

The air was warm, and the sky was clear. It was the perfect night to go stargazing if you were into that sort of mind-numbing thing.

Marcus was not.

The only time he stared up at the stars was when he was on his back, being ridden by a chick.

Or he fell and, unintentionally, ended up staring up at the stars.

If it weren't for those two scenarios, Marcus couldn't give a crap how bright the stars were shining in the sky.

Watching where he stepped, he made his way deeper into the trees behind the bar. He needed to take a piss and didn't feel the need to share this experience with the fifteen or so people enjoying drinks by the bonfire.

Some things just didn't require an audience.

Believing he had found the perfect pissing spot, he began unbuttoning his jeans, then pulled out his dick.

The air felt cool around the length of his cock. He gave it a few tugs, stretching it out to avoid any unwanted dribble on his jeans or boots.

Being a guy was not all rainbows and roses. When taking a piss, men needed to consider length, distance, wind, and backsplash.

Taking a piss was like doing hard math.

There were so many factors that one had to consider.

Not to mention the effects of alcohol. Sometimes that fucker snuck up on you, altering reality or causing sudden shifts in the gravitational pull. That shit could cause you to immediately lose your balance—nothing more embarrassing than falling to the left midstream.

Holding his cock, he closed his eyes and waited for his bladder to relax.

Any second now...

"Need a hand with that?" an annoyingly flirty voice asked.

Marcus opened one of his eyes, only to be greeted by the smiling, horny face of the succubus who had been staying with him these past few days.

"No. I've been taking a piss on my own since I was four."

The young man ignored him and continued to stalk toward him.

Marcus gripped his dick harder and commanded his bladder to release.

What was it waiting for?

"Yeah, but since then, your meat has gotten a whole lot heavier. We wouldn't want you pulling a muscle while holding on to that big, massive thing."

Marcus never really thought of himself as having a huge dick. He knew it was larger than most men's, and he had received plenty of compliments about its size since he'd first discovered girls. But he didn't go around bragging about it.

He had more important things to worry about than the size of the meat between his legs.

"I think my muscles are big enough that I don't need to worry about injuring myself. Now bug off and leave me in peace."

Marcus closed his eyes and listened to the gentle stream as it hit the dirt just inches from his feet.

God, why did taking a piss after drinking feel so fucking good?

Once his bladder was empty, Marcus opened his eyes, only to find Gavin standing a foot away from him, his eyes locked on his junk.

"Seriously, dude, you've got issues," Marcus said, shaking his dick and giving it a few tugs to get rid of any clinger-oners.

"The only issue I have is that I'm dying to swallow that cock of yours, and here you are playing hard to get."

Staring into the hungry eyes of his stalker, Marcus wondered why the boy was so focused on him rather than on any of the hundreds of other gay men who would gladly drop their drawers and feed him their meat.

Gavin wasn't a bad-looking guy by any means. In fact, his puffy red lips and slicked-up tongue would be perfect for slobbering all over any man's junk.

Slowly, Marcus's eyes slid down Gavin's throat.

Did he enjoy deep-throating cock?

Of course he did. A mouth like that was made to be used.

He wondered what Gavin sounded like, choking and gagging on a big one as he forced his way down.

Did he breathe through his nose? Or take quick gasps of air between mouthfuls of a man's thick rod?

Marcus wasn't sure.

He bet that Gavin was a moaner. He looked like a guy who enjoyed showing his partner just how much he loved swallowing cock. Perhaps he even enjoyed having his head held down as his partner throat-fucked the shit out of him.

Yes, Gavin looked like the type of guy who enjoyed getting it rough.

A moan escaped Gavin.

Marcus's eyes snapped up, locking onto his partially open mouth. His tongue slowly dragged itself along his lower lip.

Jesus, the boy looked so fuckin' turned on.

Then, Marcus glanced down at what had the boy's attention.

Without even realizing it, Marcus had been stroking his dick while thinking about Gavin's cock-sucking abilities. His dick was now rock solid and pointing right at the horny little twink.

"Looks like someone could use a release," Gavin said, stepping forward and taking Marcus's dick in his hand.

His hands felt warm and smooth.

Foreign, yet familiar.

Marcus took a step back, moving away from the spot he had just finished taking a piss in.

Gavin followed, still holding on to his shaft like he was afraid he might lose it in the dark.

Marcus swallowed as the boy took another step closer to him.

What was happening?

Their eyes were locked together, trapped in a heated force neither of them understood.

Why hadn't he pulled away from Gavin's grip?

He wasn't gay. He'd never felt the desire to feel another man's body pressed up against his. Yet, here he was, locked in a passionate stare with a young man who craved his dick.

Marcus had never fooled around with a guy before.

Yes, he'd been hit on before, and guys have made it very clear that they were willing to suck his dick if he ever wanted to explore that side of his sexuality. But until today, he'd never actually considered the offer.

Staring into Gavin's big blue eyes, he wondered what

the boy's face would look like, all blissed out and swallowing his cock?

Would he look all desperate and needy? Would he come undone while worshipping him like the sex god that he was?

Why was he even wondering these things?

Oh yeah, because his dick was rock solid, and it was very clear what it wanted—Gavin's mouth wrapped around its surface.

Marcus's lips pulled back in a wicked grin.

He placed his hand on Gavin's head, then slowly pushed him down to his knees.

The boy's face lit up when he realized that Marcus was giving him permission to suck his dick.

Pushing his jeans down around his thick thighs, Marcus watched as Gavin wrapped his hand around the base, taking in the size and girth of the meat before him.

He swore he heard Gavin whimper.

Lips parting, Gavin slowly dragged his tongue along the underside of Marcus's cock.

A groan escaped Marcus.

Fuck, the boy's tongue felt so fuckin' good along his cock.

Moving his hand to the back of Gavin's head, Marcus guided him down on his cock.

Warm, wet heat surrounded his shaft, moving lower as the boy took him all in.

"That's right. Take it all in," Marcus whispered, watching as his dick disappeared inch by inch into the heat of his mouth. "Be a good boy and take Daddy's dick."

A sinful moan came from Gavin's throat. Apparently, the boy really enjoyed the father/son role-play.

Twisting his fingers through the mess of black hair, Marcus began guiding Gavin's head, working his mouth into a steady rhythm, bobbing up and down on his rock-hard cock.

Fuck, the boy's mouth felt so fuckin' good. Like he was born to suck dick and needed it more than oxygen.

Moaning and slurping, Gavin worked over Marcus's dick like a cock-sucking virtuoso.

Was this how all gay men sucked dick? If so, why had he wasted all these years getting half-ass blow jobs from subpar women?

This was getting too much.

Marcus needed more. His alpha-male urge to dominate was taking control.

"Oh yeah. Fuck that's good," Marcus growled, grabbing Gavin by the head with both hands. "Open that throat for me," Marcus ordered as he rammed his cock into Gavin's hungry, wet hole.

Gavin's eyes dilated, clearly turned on by the sudden surge of aggression.

"Now I'm going to show you how Shadow Vipers fuck."

Letting out a snarl, Marcus began fucking the boy's mouth like it was his own personal sex toy. He paid no attention to the boy's breathing or tears as they began sliding from the corners of his eyes.

Gavin moaned and gasped, and struggled to breathe as he was force-fed Marcus's dick.

The whole thing was rough and violent, and everything that Marcus loved.

Staring up at Marcus, Gavin's eyes were so blissed out. He used his hand to jerk the length of Marcus's shaft as he did his best to accept every thrust, every deep pump that man forced into his mouth.

"Oh, you're such a good boy. Do you like taking all of Daddy's meat? Do you like it when he forces you to choke on that hog as he has his way with that fucking mouth of yours?"

Gavin's eyes dilated even more as he let out a moan and hungrily slurped down on what was given to him.

Marcus couldn't take much more of it. His mouth felt so good, swallowing him all the way down to the base before using his hands to work over his balls.

The boy was incredible.

"Fuck, babe. I'm getting so close," Marcus huffed, as he continued his assault on his newest favorite sex toy.

"Mmm, give me that load." Gavin gasped, popping off his dick quickly before diving back down and swallowing it whole.

Throwing his head back, Marcus felt his balls tighten seconds before his orgasm slammed into him.

"Fuck!" Marcus growled, slamming his hips forward as

Gavin grabbed hold of his ass and held him firmly in place while he swallowed his load.

Lights flashed before his eyes as Marcus unloaded. He tightened his grip on Gavin's hair as the boy continued to swallow every last drop.

There was something extremely sexy about a partner who swallowed your load. It was their way of saying they just couldn't get enough of you and worshipped everything about you.

Only when his body stopped spasming did Gavin finally release his death-like grip on Marcus's butt.

Smiling up at him, Gavin wiped his bottom lip, then stood up like he was the luckiest man in the world.

"Mmm. Thanks for the protein shake, Daddy." Gavin beamed as he tucked Marcus's spent cock back into his underwear and pulled up his jeans. "Can't wait to do that again!"

Marcus's vision came back into focus. "What? Next time?"

But he was already walking back toward the bonfire.

"There will be no next time," Marcus shouted, not knowing whether he didn't hear him or was just choosing to ignore him.

No, this was just a one-time blow job.

Two horny men blowing a load—well, one blowing a load while the other walked away happy as a pig in shit.

He wasn't gay, and he wasn't going to get involved with his latest assignment. Nothing good could come of it.

"Gavin?" Marcus called, watching as the boy continued to ignore him. "This isn't happening again." It sounded more like a question than the actual statement he meant it to be.

This time, Gavin threw his hand up in the air and twiddled his fingers as he stepped out into the clearing.

That little fucker was going to be the death of him. Why didn't he ever listen?

17

MARCUS

He had his dick sucked by a dude.

Staring up at the spinning fan above his bed, Marcus wondered how this had happened.

He had gone into the brush to take a leak, then the next thing he knew, he was shooting his load down Gavin's throat.

Marcus ran his hand through his hair as he continued to stare up at the spinning blades.

Did this make him gay? Bi?

Or was he just another horny straight dude looking to get his balls drained?

College dudes exchanged "brojobs" all the time, didn't they?

College dudes.

What a bunch of fuckin' wimps.

Every time he saw them working out at his gym, he just

wanted to go over and punch them in their perfect, straight teeth.

They were either drooling over themselves as they flexed their muscles in the mirrors around them. Or they were filming themselves, then checking their post every fifteen seconds to see if they got any likes.

Marcus wanted to show them his likes—right between their fucking teeth.

The gym was a place to work out, not admire yourself in the mirror like some small-dicked college jock, trying to validate his existence through the power of social media.

On second thought, just because college jocks exchanged "brojobs" wasn't a reason to confirm he wasn't gay. He was pretty sure all those "college jocks" were secretly gay for gay men's dick.

Getting back to the face-dicking he had given Gavin earlier this evening. Yup, he was pretty sure that his dick was trying to tell him something.

First, he had never been so fuckin' hard in his entire life.

Second, he had never enjoyed a blow job the way he had when Gavin was going down on him.

Was it the boy's skills? Was it the public setting? Or was it something deeper?

Whatever it was, he kind of wanted to experience it once again.

But should he?

He wasn't gay. Was he maybe bi?

Nikolai and Caden had both thought they were straight as well, but look at them now.

Dick swallowers all the way.

Was he just like them? Discovering late in life that gay sex was the way to go?

Or had he always been into dudes but just hadn't really thought about it?

Letting out a breath, he turned to glance at the clock on his nightstand.

Two a.m.

Fuck this. He threw the sheet off his body and got out of bed.

The moment he opened his bedroom door, he froze.

Sitting against the wall, just outside the door, was Gavin, puppy in lap, stroking his head.

"Oh, hey," Gavin said, suddenly startled.

Anger and guilt flashed through Marcus, pulling him in different directions. Anger at the piece of shit who had caused this. And guilt because he had closed his bedroom door, essentially telling the boy he wasn't welcome.

"Still can't sleep?" Marcus asked, standing in the doorway in nothing but his underwear. This was quickly becoming his dress of choice.

Gavin shook his head, staring down at the puppy nestled in his lap.

Marcus hated seeing him like this. He stuck out his hand and offered it to the boy.

Reluctantly, Gavin took it and let Marcus help him to his feet.

"Hop into bed. I'll get us some bottles of water," Marcus instructed.

He nodded, then headed into Marcus's bedroom.

"And the dog sleeps on the outside of us. I don't want no nasty doggy ass pressed up against me while I sleep," Marcus barked from the kitchen. He grabbed two bottles, then made his way back to his bedroom.

When he got back, Gavin was already in bed, lying on the left side with the puppy cuddled up in his arms. Marcus placed one bottle on Gavin's nightstand, then walked around the bed and placed the other bottle on his.

He wasn't thirsty anymore.

Lifting the sheet, Marcus slid in next to Gavin. He lay there for a minute, wondering whether he should say something.

"I really hate that I've become like this," Gavin whispered, his back still to Marcus.

"Like what?" Marcus asked, propping himself up on one elbow.

"Like *this.* A chicken shit. Every time I close my eyes, I see his smiling face glaring down at me in the dark. I was never like this. So weak and pathetic."

Marcus slid in closer and wrapped his arm around Gavin and the puppy.

"Hey, it's not your fault. You survived something traumatic, so it's only natural that you'll feel scared and vulnerable. I hoped that buying you that puppy might help to comfort you. I'm starting to realize that you won't feel completely safe until Sheriff Burke captures that monster."

Gavin nodded.

"I just keep thinking how close I came to being killed. The man had me alone... in his house. He drugged me and was basically steps away from slitting my throat."

Marcus tightened his grip on Gavin. He understood what the boy was saying. He wasn't sure what else he could do, other than letting him sleep in his bed at night.

Nuzzling his chin into Gavin's neck, Marcus leaned in close and whispered into his ear, "You're safe now. I won't let anything bad happen to you, ever." He wasn't sure if he could promise *ever*, but he was damn sure going to try. "Tomorrow, I'll call Sheriff Burke to see how the investigation's going."

"Thank you," Gavin whispered as he relaxed his back into Marcus's chest.

This was only temporary, Marcus told himself. Once Sheriff Burke and his team caught the Valentine Killer, Gavin would feel safe once again.

And if Burke couldn't find the bastard?

Well, that's when Marcus and the boys went hunting.

"So, you got nothing?" Marcus growled into the phone,

trying his best to keep his voice down while he bit Sheriff Burke's head off through the phone at the same time.

Gavin was still sleeping, and Marcus didn't want to wake him. Lord knows the kid needed some sleep.

"We're getting there. We swept through his house and now know the killer's real name is Clive Trent, and he used to work as a drilling engineer before he got let go six months ago. I wouldn't say that was nothing," Burke argued through the phone.

The killer had given Gavin a false name when he met him—*typical for someone who planned on murdering you a few hours later. Why share your real name?*

The more he talked to Burke, the more he wanted to shove this Clive's face through a wall.

Until this asshole was caught, Gavin would never feel safe again.

"What about other potential victims? Don't you want to capture this guy before he snatches up another victim?"

"Of course we do!" Sheriff Burke barked back. "I'm sorry this is taking so long, but we have steps that we need to follow. Otherwise, even if we do arrest him, the courts won't find him guilty. We need this man locked up."

That was the same thing Nikolai's better half, Reid, told Marcus when they were trying to take down a human trafficking ring not too long ago. The criminal justice system sucked and seemed to work only for criminals, not victims. That wasn't right at all.

"Trust me, Burke, you want to find this guy before I

do," Marcus snarled. The thought of that monster almost extinguishing the lights of such a sweet, funny, and annoying twink filled Marcus's veins with rage.

There was a long pause on the other end of the phone.

Was Burke actually considering his offer?

"I'll keep you posted on any progress we make on our end. Let me know if the boy becomes too much for you to handle."

"No, that's not it. The boy is fine, and he's safe. I just want to catch this scumbag before he hurts anyone else. Monsters like this guy don't deserve to be breathing fresh air." *They don't deserve to be breathing at all.*

Marcus let out a sigh.

"Just let me know what I can do on my end to help you out with your case. Gavin is doing well here, so don't worry about him."

Burke let out a chuckle.

"He's annoying the shit out of you, isn't he?"

Marcus looked over his shoulder toward his bedroom, half expecting Gavin to be standing there, watching him.

"More than you know," Marcus noted with no heat in his voice.

The truth was, he kind of liked having Gavin around. The spitfire, little bundle of energy, always found a way to keep him on his toes. There were many similarities between Gavin and his brother, Ace, and having Gavin in his home just felt... natural. Warm and inviting.

Marcus couldn't put his finger on it, but being around

the guy somehow made him feel whole again, like he wasn't missing something from his life.

He felt needed and wanted, and the way that those blue eyes looked up at him while they were swallowing his dick... was pure *want* and *desire*.

Desire.

Marcus always thought of himself as rough and tough, a true alpha male when it came to getting naked in the bedroom.

But seeing the way Gavin looked at him... made him feel so...

"Who are you talking to?" a groggy voice asked from behind him.

Marcus couldn't help the tiny grin that pulled at his face. His boy was awake.

Ending the call, Marcus placed his cell phone down on the kitchen counter.

"Sheriff Burke. Just getting an update from the guy."

Gavin rounded the counter, with the puppy following at his heels. The little guy was stumbling over himself, trying to nip at his master's feet.

"And?" Gavin asked, pressing his arms against the counter as he waited for an update.

"And... they're making good headway. It shouldn't be too much longer."

He didn't have the heart to tell Gavin that Burke and team were fucking useless, and that the monster of his dreams was still out lurking in the shadows.

No, for now, it was best to keep things positive.

The Shadow Vipers would continue to protect the boy, while Marcus secretly worked out a plan to hunt down and take that motherfucker out.

It seemed that lately, the Shadow Vipers were in the business of unaliving people.

Well, at least they were all bad guys who deserved every last stab, bite, explosion, or poison that they received.

Staring into those gentle, vulnerable eyes, Marcus knew he was treading in dangerous territory. He needed to protect the boy, but he also couldn't help that awkward feeling that was beginning to grow just beneath his rib cage.

"So, what do you want for breakfast? I can make eggs and sausage?"

Gavin gave a tired groan.

"Just kidding. I'll make you a kale smoothie and lawn clipping salad."

The sweet sound of Gavin chuckling filled the room.

"Sounds delicious."

Yes, it sounded delicious... didn't it? He should probably buy a vegetarian cookbook to finally figure out what those weirdoes ate. If he was going to keep this one fed and entertained, he should probably know what they regularly consumed.

He turned to his cupboard, opened it, and started rummaging inside.

18

MARCUS

Twenty-Seven Years Ago

"Marcus, get in the car, sweety. It's time to go home," Marcus's mother called from the open window of her broken-down, piece-of-shit car that was crawling around on its last life.

Marcus ignored his mother. "It's your turn, Billy."

He didn't want to go home. The streetlights weren't even on, and he was just about to beat his best friend at knives.

Holding his hand flat against the concrete, Marcus waited for his buddy to pick up the knife and begin stabbing between his spread fingers. Marcus had already beaten his other two friends, who chickened out and cried "Mercy" when Marcus brought the blade down between their third or fourth fingers.

Marcus decided to be nice and let his best friend start off as the stabber. His friend just had to stab between his fingers until the song playing finished or Marcus said the word "mercy."

"It's your turn, Billy. Or are you too chicken to try?"

His best friend swallowed hard, and he stared at Marcus's spread-out hand.

"But... what if I..." Billy began before being cut off by one more of Marcus's mother's bellows from the car.

"Get yo stinkin' assss in tha car, right now... you piece of fuckin' shit!"

His mother's words were slurred once again. Not that her words weren't on most days.

Marcus was used to it. It was just the way his mother always sounded.

"Argh! Fine!" Marcus shouted, jumping up from the ground and snatching up his blade in the process. "I'll see you guys tomorrow," Marcus said as he turned to walk down Billy's long driveway and hopped inside his mother's car.

Well, technically, it was Daddy's, but Mama always liked to use the car when she was heading out to buy some more alcohol.

"It's abou—fuckin' time you got in da fuckin' car," his mama snapped, not even waiting for Marcus to get fully seated in the car before peeling away from Billy's house.

Marcus huffed and folded his arms across his chest.

"Why did you come pick me up? It's not even dark yet. I'm twelve years old. I can walk home by myself."

"Mama needs to stop at the store real quick," his mother stated as she blew through a stop sign, narrowly missing a car turning right.

"To buy more booze, I bet."

Her head snapped in his direction.

"You watch that mouth of yours, you little shit."

A horn blared from somewhere behind them.

His mother made a right onto Maple Drive, then pressed down hard on the gas as she rushed toward the liquor store. She was in a rush because the store closed at eight, and it was already ten minutes until closing.

"Is Pops home?" Marcus asked, clicking his seat belt into place as he stared out the front windshield.

"How the fuck should I know? He's probably off fuckin' one of his whores or getting shit-faced down in the bar."

Marcus shrugged. He really didn't give two shits about either of his parents. They were both mega pieces of shit, and Marcus couldn't wait until he was old enough to move out on his own.

He couldn't stand the constant fighting and arguing or the broken beer bottles that lay smashed on the kitchen floor.

His mother took another hard right, this time almost hitting an elderly woman who was trying to cross the road.

"Mom, you need to slow down, you're driving like a crazy person," Marcus said, reaching for the stereo to turn up the music.

His mother turned and slapped him across the cheek.

"Don't you talk to me like that!"

The car swerved as Marcus raised his arm to defend himself.

"Well, you're drivin' like a psycho bitch, you fuckin' drunk!"

His mother screamed at him as she took her hands off the wheel and reached across the seat, slapping him with both hands.

"Mama! Don't—"

The world went black around him.

The next thing Marcus remembered was waking up to the sound of hundreds of machines beeping. Some people were crying. Others were shouting and arguing.

The throbbing pain in his head was the only thing that Marcus could focus on.

"I think he's awake," someone said.

"Son? Can you hear me?" a male voice spoke as a hand dropped down on his shoulder.

"Ye-yeah?" Marcus managed to get out.

His eyes slowly opened to the sight of two police officers standing next to his bed.

He was in the hospital.

"Wh-where's my mom?"

The two police officers looked at each other as a nurse came rushing to his bed.

"Try not to move, sweety. You were in an accident and have a broken arm. Your dad is on his way," the nurse with the bright red hair said as she checked out his monitors and wrote something down on a clipboard.

"Where's my mom?" Marcus asked once again. She was probably off at the liquor store buying another bottle before they closed.

More silence.

Marcus turned his head to the bed next to him.

There, hooked up to all these machines and tubes, was his mother. Her eyes were closed, and she wasn't moving.

"Mom?" Marcus called. "Mom?"

"Your mom is in bad shape, kid," one of the police officers said, giving him one of those sympathetic looks that most adults gave him when they saw him standing next to his mother.

It was sympathy. A look that said they were sorry, but there was nothing that they could do.

Marcus fucking hated them. He hated them all. Every fucking piece of shit who saw his parents and didn't do a goddamn thing. Fucking useless. They all were.

"Is she dead?"

No one said a word.

"Try and get some sleep, son," the other office said, giving him one of those looks as well. "You'll need your rest to heal."

His mother died sometime during the night. Marcus never knew whether his father made it to the hospital in time to see his wife one last time before she died. It wasn't until the morning, when Marcus woke up next to an empty bed, that he found out that his mother had passed away.

Marcus was never sure how he really felt about his mother's passing. Yes, she was his mother and gave birth to him. But she was also a mean alcoholic who never seemed to give a shit about him or his bastard of a father.

It was shortly after his mother's death that Marcus made a promise to himself. If he ever got married and had a family of his own, he would be there for them. Protecting them and always doing what was best for his family.

He hoped that one day he would be able to keep that promise to himself.

19

GAVIN

Laughter erupted around the room as Lucas fell to his knees, imitating one of the many mishaps he had endured this past week while trying to educate his young students.

As Gavin was quickly learning, Lucas was not the most... gracious when it came to standing on two feet.

"Oh my god. You're hilarious." Gavin chuckled, lifting his sangria and taking another sip. "And I have to say, these drinks are fucking good!"

Gavin lifted his glass and waited for Ace and Lucas to join him in a cheer.

"Ace is the master of sangrias. He got me hooked when I first moved to town," Lucas explained, crawling along the floor and reaching for his glass.

"That's right. I heard that you moved here from LA. How was that?" Gavin asked, taking a sip of his drink.

"It was the best decision I ever made. I got out of an abusive relationship, met this hunky, straight biker dude, then somehow ended up becoming best friends with this Latino freak who insists on getting us drunk!"

Lucas raised his glass to his best friend and shot him an air kiss as well.

Sitting in Marcus's living room, enjoying Saturday night drinks with his two new besties, Gavin almost felt normal.

It had been almost two weeks since the Valentine Killer had almost ended Gavin's life, and the police appeared to be no closer to finding the madman.

Gavin still slept in Marcus's room each night, but they hadn't fooled around since that blow job in the woods.

It wasn't for lack of trying. Gavin kept grinding his ass into Marcus's lap as they cuddled while they slept, to which Marcus usually just growled, then turned his raging hard-on away from Gavin's horny hole.

He even tried accidentally walking out of the shower, naked, hoping that might get a rise out of the growly biker. All it managed to get was a set of wide eyes and a quick exit from the bedroom they shared.

Who knows. Maybe the man wasn't interested.

"God!" Gavin exhaled sharply as he threw his head back against the sofa. "I'm so frickin' bored! I miss going out to clubs and dancing and finding hot, sexy men to grind up against and flirt with till the wee hours of the morning."

Ace and Lucas both looked at him.

"Well, the dancing sounds fun. But the grinding with strange men sounds kind of like a death sentence for those poor innocent souls," Ace noted.

Gavin gave him an awkward look. *Was he that undesirable that it was a death sentence for men he made out with?*

"Yeah. If Caden or Blade ever found out that we were out dancing with other men, they would go homicidal," Lucas added.

Whew! That Gavin could handle.

"They'd probably beat their asses till they were breathing through an oxygen tube..." Ace continued.

"Then they'd take us home... and..." Lucas began, swallowing hard as if turned on by the thought.

"Fuck us till we can't see straight," Ace finally finished for his best friend.

Both their heads snapped toward Gavin.

"We're going out!" both shouted in unison, smiles practically swallowing their heads.

"What?" Gavin asked, suddenly wondering what he had gotten himself into.

"I'm ordering us a rideshare," Ace blurted, as Lucas jumped to his feet, rushing to Ace's old bedroom. He emerged a few minutes later with a handful of clothing, which he quickly began distributing.

Gavin held up the black mesh shirt he'd been given, wondering what he was supposed to do with this... *loosely* held together article of clothing.

"Quick, put that on. Our ride will be here in ten," Ace ordered, pulling off the rock T-shirt he had been wearing and replacing it with a crop top that said, "Naughty When Nice."

Fifteen minutes later, they all squished into the back of a rideshare and were headed to one of the bars that doubled as a gay bar about thirty minutes away.

New Mexico wasn't exactly known for its thriving gay scene, so bars like these existed to provide the queer community and their supporters with a safe place to gather and hang out.

"Oh my god, this place is amazing!" Gavin exclaimed as they walked across the club and found an empty spot to stand next to the bar.

Ace took a sip of his martini and smiled back at Gavin.

"I know it's not the fancy clubs you're used to in the big cities, but it's got music, people, and loads of cheap drinks!"

"That it does," Lucas agreed, throwing his arm around Ace and leaning in to kiss his cheek.

These guys were great.

Having Ace and Lucas as friends really helped him feel less lonely and almost made him feel normal again. These last few weeks had been a whirlwind of emotions, and being out with his friends who genuinely seemed to care about him and his well-being had his heart swelling.

He had finally found a place where he belonged. For

real. And not the fictional façade he created and posted for everyone each day.

Having Marcus and Ace and Lucas in his life, and now his puppy, he almost felt... happy.

"Hey, let's take a picture," Gavin shouted, wanting to capture this moment, this feeling, so he would never forget it.

He held out his phone and switched it to selfie mode.

The three of them leaned close to each other, like lifelong friends having the time of their lives. They all held up their drinks while making funny faces.

Gavin snapped a few photos, laughing and smiling and secretly wishing that a big growly someone was there with them. The more he got to know Marcus, the more his heart craved his attention.

"Let's go dance!" Lucas shouted, reaching for both of their hands.

"I'll meet you guys there in a sec," Gavin said, opening his social media apps as he tried to decide which one of their photos he wanted to post.

Lucas nodded to him as he grabbed Ace's hand and pulled him toward the dance floor.

Smiling, Gavin wanted to share this feeling... this emotion... with all his followers. They deserved that. That was why they followed him. They wanted to be a part of his life. His journey. And Gavin was feeling way too good at the moment, not to want to share his joy with the world.

It had been almost a week since he last posted

anything. His fans must be wondering where he was and why he had gone radio silent.

When he finally opened the app, he couldn't believe the number of comments and direct messages he'd gotten from followers asking where he was and why he had suddenly disappeared.

Some theorized he'd been arrested, while others claimed he'd checked himself into rehab, swearing that their cousin's best friend's mom had seen him at their rehab facility. That one made him laugh, considering the post he was about to make.

Others thanked God that the poser had finally given up and gone back to his sad and pathetic life, pretending he was an "instagay," seeking attention and spreading his poor attempt at being relevant and important.

Got to love the trolls.

It's sad that people have nothing else going on in their lives, so they spend their time trying to cut others down, trying to feel better about their own sad, pathetic lives.

Whatever. He didn't need to entertain people like that.

Selecting a bunch of photos they had just taken, Gavin added some catchy captions, referring to the club as a hidden gem in an undisclosed location.

Yes, Gavin was still around and kicking. He was having one of the best times while hanging out with his two new besties.

Closing out the app, Gavin picked up what was left of his drink and jogged out onto the dance floor to enjoy the rest of the evening, dancing with his new best friends.

They laughed, they joked, and they took wild and stupid selfies.

There was no thought of killers. No thought of parents who couldn't care less whether he lived or died.

Just friends, being friends.

It wasn't until the ride home, three hours later, that Gavin decided to check his socials to see how his fans were reacting to his instant return.

Most followers were happy—and relieved—to see him back on social media. They loved him and couldn't wait to hear more about his new best friends and the fabulous club he was out at. It had a western gay bar, grunge feel about it and would be perfect for those down-to-earth queers who loved a chill and cozy environment.

Switching over to his direct messages, Gavin scanned through the ocean of messages, searching for any that sounded kind of interesting.

Next to him, Ace adjusted his head on Gavin's shoulder as he slept. On the other side of him, Lucas smiled like a love-struck puppy as he texted his boyfriend, Caden.

He loved his two new best friends.

As he scrolled through the string of endless messages, Gavin's fingers stopped when he spotted a message from RomanceLoverXXX. It was a username that he had never seen before, but there was something about the beginning of his message that caught Gavin's attention.

RomanceLoverXXX: ***It's nice to see you smiling again. I was worried that perhaps I had taken that away from you as well. I hear that you're not sleeping so well these days. I'm sorry. I have that effect on people... By the way, love the meshed shirt. Really brings out that KILLER body of yours. See you soon, VK.***

Gavin's heart stopped in his chest.

He stared at the last two letters... VK.

Valentine Killer?

Was it a message from him?

It had to be.

Oh my god. He suddenly felt sick to his stomach.

The killer had been watching him. How else would he have known that he wasn't sleeping well at night? Then another terrifying thought—he knows where he is.

Gavin felt his heart begin beating fast in his chest.

He glanced up at the driver currently taking them home.

Was that him?

Had they gotten into a car with a killer?

It was suddenly becoming hard for Gavin to breathe.

"What is it?" Ace asked, lifting his head from Gavin's shoulder, appearing to sense the sudden shift in his friend's demeanor.

"I... I..." Gavin's mind was blank. He didn't know what to do or say. His body locked up as his hands began to shake.

Confused and worried, Ace took the phone from Gavin's hand and glanced down at the message.

His mouth dropped open when he read it.

Locking Gavin's phone, Ace dropped it into his lap.

"We're almost home," Ace said, wrapping his arm around Gavin and pulling him into his chest. "You're safe. You're with us. My brother will know what to do."

Lucas glanced over at Ace, silently asking what was going on.

Gavin just sat there, letting Ace hold him close.

The killer had found him. He'd been watching him for weeks.

He wasn't safe.

None of them were safe.

Gavin closed his eyes and wished for Marcus.

20

MARCUS

The commotion at the front door had Marcus jerking awake and reaching for the gun hidden under the sofa.

“Marcus! Where are you?” he heard his brother, Ace, shout from the hallway.

What was going on?

Marcus took a step forward before Ace, Lucas, and Gavin appeared in the hallway.

“Where the hell were you guys?” Marcus asked, pissed that they hadn’t left a note or answered any of the hundred texts he had sent them.

They had left a mess in the living room, a graveyard of empty bottles of wine and random clothing thrown all over the furniture.

Marcus would have been concerned if it hadn’t been for the text Caden sent him letting him know that Lucas had been sexting him, while the others were busy dancing on the dance floor.

Which dance floor? Caden had no idea.

"Marcus! He found him," Ace rushed, helping a clearly distraught Gavin into the living room.

"He's going to kill me," Gavin muttered, his eyes unfocused and staring at the floor. "He's going to hack me to bits and leave a card in my pocket." The boy was speaking to himself, apparently unaware of the people standing around him.

"Gavin, are you alright?" Marcus asked, grabbing him by the face and staring into his unfocused eyes.

The sound of his voice seemed to jerk Gavin out of whatever trauma he was experiencing. His eyes came back into focus and settled on his with a sudden gasp.

"Marcus!" the boy cried, lunging at him and wrapping his arms around his body. "He found me. He's here. He's going to kill me."

What? The boy wasn't making any sense.

"Please don't let him kill me," Gavin begged, sobbing into his chest.

That plea broke Marcus's heart.

"What? What's going on?" Marcus asked, holding Gavin tight while looking over at his brother.

Ace held up Gavin's phone so he could read the message on the screen.

Rage suddenly flooded Marcus's system.

The fucker was here. Watching Gavin. Right under their very noses.

Running his hand over the back of Gavin's head, Marcus tried to comfort him.

"Shhh, it's alright, Gav. I got you now. You're safe here, with us." Marcus looked over at Ace, who was already on his phone, calling Blade and the rest of the crew. Ace walked into the kitchen so Gavin wouldn't overhear what he was saying on the phone.

"You trust me, right, Gav?" Marcus asked, holding his breath as he waited for an answer.

Gavin nodded into his chest as he clung to him with a strength Marcus had never felt before.

"And you know, I would rather die than let anything bad ever happen to you?"

Gavin nodded once again without lifting his face.

Marcus caught Lucas looking over at him, taking note of the pledge he was making to the man he held in his arms.

"I need you to trust me and know that you are safe here in this house. The guys and I will be right here with you at all times. We won't let this bastard anywhere near you." Marcus hoped that at least some of his words would get through to the terrified boy, help comfort him, and reassure him that everything was going to be okay.

Sniffling, Gavin nodded his head once again.

"Thank you, Marcus. You always make me feel safe when I'm around you."

Relief set in knowing that he was getting through to the boy. He held him close, caressing the back of Gavin's head as he watched Ace walk back into the room.

"Blade and the others are on their way over," Ace explained.

"Good. Call Alexis and Jake and tell them what's going on. I want all Vipers on alert. I want their eyes and ears open. I want to know if there are any new guys here in this town, and if there are, where are they staying? This here is top priority. I want this fucker found, and I want him found now," Marcus growled, feeling the beast inside him stir.

Someone had stepped into his town and threatened the people he loved. Gavin, Ace, Lucas, Blade, and all the members of the Shadow Vipers were under his protection. A threat to one was a threat to them all.

This would not stand, and an example needed to be made of this so-called serial killer.

If it was a fight this guy wanted, it was a fight he was going to get.

He might be kind and loving to those he cared about—or so he was told—but he was also mean and ruthless when it came to protecting those he loved. Just asked anyone who'd betrayed him... if you could find their body, or any part of them that still functioned.

It was time for the Shadow Vipers to go hunting.

~

An hour later, the house was filled with all of Marcus's brothers and sisters. Every space of the living room and kitchen was taken over by one member or another.

Marcus was glad they were all here. He wanted to get everyone up to speed and make sure everyone was safe.

"Okay, I think we're all here," Marcus began, glancing around the room to be sure that all of his crew was present. "As many of you know, we've been protecting Gavin for the past several weeks. What some of you might not know is that we have been protecting Gavin from a serial killer."

There were a few gasps as some crew members discovered the true nature of the duty they were performing. Most knew they were protecting Gavin from someone, but they didn't know the details exactly.

They all glanced over at Gavin, who was sitting against the wall between Ace and Lucas, with the puppy whining in his lap. He could sense that something was wrong and kept licking Gavin's hand as he slowly caressed his fur.

Next to Ace stood Blade, casually flipping his favorite blade in his hand, while Caden stood protectively on the other side of Lucas, arms crossed against his chest, his eyes scanning the room for any sign of danger.

Gavin sat in the center, seemingly unaware of the dangerous crew standing guard around him.

"The Valentine Killer, to be exact," Marcus added, watching as his crew began to whisper around him. "Tonight, we received a message that appears to indicate that the killer is in town and has been watching us for quite some time."

Nikolai stepped forward, his fists clenched in anger. "If he has, he's a dead man. No one threatens my family and gets away with it," Nikolai growled in a thick Russian accent. His accent always grew thicker the angrier he seemed to get.

"That's why I asked you all here tonight. First, to make sure that everyone was safe and aware of the situation; second, to come up with a plan to hunt down this psychopath and take him out once and for all."

Marcus had given up on trying to capture and arrest this piece of shit. This was personal now, and the only way to ensure that his family remained safe was to take the bastard out and eliminate the threat indefinitely.

"We're with you, boss," Blade added, nodding his head at his brother-in-law. He was always ready for a fight when it came to family.

"What do you need, boss?" Damian, one of the Viper crew members and a worker at the bar, asked, tucking his hands under his armpits and waiting for his boss to give them instructions.

"Tonight, you're all going to sleep here, then tomorrow morning, we're going to come up with a plan." Marcus looked over at Nikolai and Midas. "You guys make sure that the house is secure. Double-check every door, window, and outside security light. Take Caden if you need an extra set of hands. Ace, start thinking of what we might need. We can't all stay here forever, so whatever solution you can think of, I'm open to suggestions."

Marcus looked over at Gavin, who now sat with his arms wrapped around his knees, holding them close to his chest as he sat on the floor rocking slowly. The puppy stared up at him, waiting patiently for his favorite person to do something with him.

The guy had been through so much these past few weeks. His once safe space had now been violated. Marcus made a pledge right there to never again leave the boy's side.

He was going to find a way to draw out this motherfucker, then end his life, one way or another.

But tonight, they were going to lock down the place, then worry about things in the morning.

Heart beating in his chest, Marcus walked over to the terrified man he had once tossed into his trunk to protect him and scooped him up into his arms.

"Puppy, come," Marcus ordered, carrying Gavin bodyguard-style down the hallway and into his bedroom.

"I'll stand guard at the door," Nikolai announced from the doorway like his own private security.

Marcus nodded without turning as he gently placed Gavin on the bed. He scooped up the puppy and dropped him into the boy's open arms.

Behind him, Nikolai closed his bedroom door.

Feeling an overwhelming need to stand guard and protect what he loved, Marcus slid into the bed and wrapped his massive body around the boy—and the puppy–protecting them both and making sure they knew they were safe and could let their guard down while they slept.

Marcus would stay awake, watching and listening, making sure everyone under his roof was safe and protected.

No one, no matter how crazy or psychotic they might be, would dare break into a house filled with armed, angry bikers just looking to get into a scrap.

21

MARCUS

Light crept into the room as the early morning sun slowly rose over the horizon. Marcus watched the beams as they slowly moved across the ceiling, tracking time as it gradually ticked by.

He wasn't sure what time it was, probably five or six in the morning. He hadn't slept, just listened to the noises around him, ready to pounce if any should become a threat.

But no threats came. Perhaps it was just enough for Marcus and his crew to know that the Valentine Killer was out there to keep the psychotic killer happily away.

Killers got off on that sort of thing, didn't they? Causing fear and panic, watching as their prey slowly unraveled... waiting... wondering... counting the minutes until that deadly blow might come. If it would come?

But Marcus was no victim. He didn't allow people to

gain power over him. He faced dangers head-on and reveled in the pain that his revenge brought out.

No. Marcus was not scared. He was simply waiting. Thinking through strategies and options, moving pieces on the chessboard of violence to see which outcomes he liked the best.

Soon, he would have his plan of attack all mapped out, making sure everyone was safe and taken care of. Because he was the leader of the Shadow Vipers. And that's what leaders did—they looked out for their crew and stepped in front of danger wherever it might be.

Pulling Gavin close to him, Marcus gently kissed the top of his head. He wasn't sure why he had done it, only that his heart was telling him he wanted to take care of the boy and make sure he felt safe and secure.

Listening to Gavin sleep, curled into his side for safety and warmth, had Marcus feeling all sorts of strange things.

It was clear that the boy trusted him. He sought him out whenever he needed comfort. That was never in question.

He knew that Gavin also had feelings for him, whether they were romantic in nature or simply a horny man's need to get himself off. Whatever the nature, Marcus enjoyed having that knowledge.

It was becoming harder and harder to keep his hands off Gavin. The draw he felt for the young man was growing stronger every day they were together.

The mischievous smile the boy got whenever he did something he knew would drive Marcus crazy.

The act of defiance whenever Marcus asked him to do something he didn't want to do. Like pick his clothes up off the floor or put the dirty dishes in the sink for washing.

The way Gavin always looked for him, making sure that Marcus was always close by, even when they were busy doing other things.

Marcus loved it. He felt needed. Wanted. Even challenged when they were having a disagreement.

There was something new and refreshing about the boy.

Everything about him was making it harder and harder not to throw the guy down on the nearest hard surface and have his way with him.

Marcus swallowed as he felt his cock begin to thicken. Good thing he was wearing jeans because popping a boner right at this moment seemed a tad inappropriate.

Gavin let out a moan and stirred against his body.

"Mmm, what time is it?" he asked softly, nuzzling his face into Marcus's side.

"It's still early. Try and get some more sleep if you can." Marcus lowered his head and gently kissed the top of his head once more.

He felt the boy smile against him.

"I like this soft side of my big protector."

Marcus squeezed him close. "I have no idea what you're talking about."

Chuckling, Gavin wrapped his arm around Marcus's stomach, clinging to him like he was the happiest person in the world. "Sure, you don't."

They lay like that for another hour before deciding they weren't going to get any more sleep that morning.

Quietly, they opened the bedroom door, only to be greeted by a smirking Russian.

"If the boy isn't walking funny, then you're doing something wrong, boss."

Marcus rolled his eyes. "I'm sure there are laws against listening behind people's bedroom doors."

Nikolai stood and stretched, reaching his arms toward the ceiling. His shirt rode up, exposing the words "Reid's Property" tattooed across his lower abs, with an arrow pointing down beneath his briefs.

"Nice tattoo," Gavin noted, walking past the bulked bouncer and pulling Marcus after him.

"Morning, guys," they announced as they entered the kitchen, where Ace and Blade were already up chatting.

"Mornin'," they answered in unison.

"Want some coffee?" Ace asked, stepping away from Blade and grabbing a mug from the kitchen cupboard.

Marcus let out a grunt, typical pre-coffee communication they were all used to by now.

"I'll get breakfast started," Blade offered, pulling items from the fridge at random.

Ace and Blade made breakfast, while Marcus and Caden passed out coffee to those who were awake.

They spent the next hour eating breakfast, spread out across the kitchen and living room.

Once everyone was done and coffees had been refilled, they all moved to the living room to discuss their plan of attack.

"I think the best place to take him out will be Marcus's cottage. It's secluded and private and draws that psychopath away from Baton and all its residents," Ace suggested.

"I think you're right," Marcus agreed. "We'll close down the bar for a few days and move all the Shadow Vipers up to the cottage. This way, everyone will be safe, and we can take out the bastard together."

The room was silent as everyone listened to Marcus's instructions.

"Actually, we might have a better chance at flushing out this guy if Gavin isn't surrounded by a mob of bikers. I know you won't like it, but leaving Gavin exposed makes him better bait in the end," Ace suggested.

"Gavin isn't bait," Marcus barked back, glaring at his younger brother for suggesting such a thing.

There was no chance in hell he was using the boy as bait. There were better ways to lure out a serial killer. They didn't need to risk Gavin's safety and possibly his life just to make things easier for them to draw him out.

"No. We aren't using him," Marcus repeated.

Gavin raised his head and locked eyes with Marcus. He was sitting between Lucas and Caden.

"You know this is the best way of luring him out. If it keeps people safe, then I'm all for being used as bait. Plus, I'll have you there to protect me."

That he did.

While Marcus didn't like the thought of dangling Gavin in front of a psychopath, like a worm on a hook, he knew that using Gavin was their best chance at success.

They needed to lure the Valentine Killer out of hiding, and getting him to voluntarily walk into a home swarming with bikers wasn't exactly the smartest of plans.

The guys were right. They needed to do it their way.

"Fine," Marcus agreed reluctantly.

"Good," Ace responded. "Blade and I will ride up to the cottage shortly to secure the place and get it ready for your arrival. You and Gavin ride up later tonight. That will give us time to shop and stock up the place so you guys won't have to. Once you settle in, a small team of us will monitor the property from a safe distance and let you know if we see anything suspicious." Ace turned to face Gavin. "We want the Valentine Killer to think that you and Marcus are hiding out at the cottage alone. Once he thinks it's safe, he will come out of hiding and try to take you. Don't worry, we will be watching the place around the clock."

"Sounds like a plan," Gavin responded.

When did his brother become such a smart cookie?

Sometime between when he first learned to talk and when he started to discover boys, Marcus guessed.

There was a reason he relied on his little brother so much. He'd be lost without the little prick.

But then something occurred to Marcus.

"Wait. No. This plan isn't going to work. How am I supposed to protect everyone when all of you are scattered across different locations?" Marcus shook his head. "Nope. It's best if everyone comes to the cottage with Gavin and me. God knows we have the room for everyone. We can figure out a way to draw this fucker out later."

All eyes moved between Marcus and Ace. A standoff was about to begin between their leader and his little brother.

Ace stepped forward.

"Marcus. I know that as the leader of the Shadow Vipers, you feel a responsibility to look after and protect all of us, but keep in mind, we are all grown-ass adults. We've all been in scraps before and taken out more gang members than we care to admit. For once in your life, let your crew take care of you. You don't need to protect us all the time. This time, we've got your back. We are the ones who are going to be protecting you."

Hearing Ace's words made it suddenly hard to swallow.

Not because he was having trouble breathing, but because there was suddenly a goddamn lump in his throat that was getting even bigger with every word his little brother spoke.

Looking around the room, he saw that everyone was nodding.

"We got you" and "It's our turn to look out for you" could be heard throughout the living room.

All these men and women, his family, his crew—they were all here for him. Standing up alongside him, ready to go to their death if needed, all so they could protect him and all those he loved.

Marcus had never felt so loved.

"You're right, Ace. You're all fully capable of taking care of yourselves. I guess I care about everyone so damn much that sometimes I forget to think about myself and what's best for the situation." Marcus stepped forward and hugged his brother. "Your plan is great."

22

GAVIN

The roar of the engine from the Harley echoed through the trees as Marcus pulled into the driveway of the cottage.

Cottage.

If you could call it that.

In reality, it was a long mansion by the lake. Three whole families could live year-round in the place and never get in each other's way.

Marcus could have all the members of his crew up at this place for weeks, and nobody would complain.

Gavin wondered how many bedrooms the place had.

"So, is this your cottage?" Gavin asked, stepping off the bike and removing his helmet.

Marcus, of course, did not use a helmet. Neither did any of the other guys in his crew. Safety was not considered hot or sexy when it came to biker life. Yet, for some reason, Gavin was forced to wear the protective gear.

Marcus looked up at the looming structure and nodded.

"Yeah. I needed a place to conduct certain... *transactions*. This place offered the privacy and space, plus wait till you see the hot tub," Marcus said with a cocky smile on his face.

"Transactions" was code for *bringing people here to kill them*, no doubt.

Gavin knew better than to ask for clarification. He was already surprised at how much crew business Marcus disclosed in front of him. He didn't exactly hide that he wasn't always law-abiding, but he also didn't go around pretending to be something he was not.

It was kind of refreshing. Most guys Gavin knew lied even more than they breathed. Yet, here Marcus was, not hiding anything from him. And for that, Gavin was grateful.

Once inside, Gavin placed the puppy down on the floor and watched as he scurried off, exploring all the dark hallways and corners around them.

They really needed to think of a name for their dog. They couldn't go around calling him "Puppy" his whole life.

Or could they?

Marcus carried their knapsacks up a wooden staircase

and down a long hallway to the primary bedroom they would be sharing.

"I'm going to take a shower and wash this ride off me," Marcus grumbled, pulling off his shirt, then undoing the top button of his jeans. "You going to be okay out here, alone?"

Gavin looked around the large bedroom, taking it all in for the first time. The whole place was overwhelming and would take him a while to get used to.

"How about I save you some water and join you in the shower?" Gavin asked, pulling off his shirt and heading toward the en suite bathroom.

He wasn't going to wait for Marcus to put up a fight or tell him why they shouldn't get naked together in the shower.

"Are you coming?" Gavin called over his shoulder as he stepped out of his pants and turned on the shower.

Before he knew it, Gavin could feel the towering presence of Marcus standing just inches behind his partially naked, slim frame.

Without turning around, he slid his underwear slowly down his body and listened as the man behind him let out a low growl.

He could almost taste the sexual tension between them —a hungry beast, watching as his delicious meal prepared to be devoured.

Stepping into the shower, Gavin watched as Marcus stepped out of his jeans, then stuck his thumbs into the top of his boxer briefs, pausing momentarily as he stared at Gavin's naked body.

The bulge between Marcus's legs shifted as the meat behind the material began to grow.

Gavin licked his bottom lip as he watched the six-foot-four hunk of man slip out of his underwear and give his semihard cock a generous tug.

Watching Marcus pull on his meat sent all of Gavin's blood directly to his cock.

How was this mountain of a man not in porn?

Holding his breath, he watched as the sexiest man he had ever seen stepped into the shower and settled next to him.

Eyes locked together, Gavin grabbed the loofah and poured some bodywash onto its surface before working it between his hands to build a nice lather.

There was no way he was ever taking his eyes off this gorgeous, naked beast of a man.

Sliding further under the water, Gavin pulled Marcus's body closer to his. Water splashed off the solid contours of Marcus's body, dripping down his nipples and then sliding across his stomach.

Gavin didn't need to look down to know that his cock was rock solid. Being this close to Marcus, naked and exposed, had every hormone firing inside him.

With great care, Gavin began soaping up Marcus's chest using the loofah. Their eyes remained locked together, as Gavin's hands continued to explore every inch of Marcus's body.

Neither said a word, just stared at each other with longing in their eyes.

In that moment, only the two of them existed. There was no murderer out to kill them, no worries of people's safety—just two grown men, locked in each other's gaze, finally embracing the feelings they had been harboring for one another over these past few weeks.

Once Marcus's chest, shoulders, and stomach were good and soapy, Gavin moved further south, grabbing Marcus's thick piece of meat with one hand, and using his other to soap up his shaft.

He watched as Marcus's eyes rolled back in his head as he worked over his cock and lathered up his balls.

Swallowing hard, Gavin tried not to moan as Marcus slid his hips forward, pumping his dick in and out of Gavin's firm grip.

Fuck. Was he really giving Marcus a hand job in the shower?

"Fuck, you're so damn hot," Gavin whispered, lowering his gaze so he could watch Marcus fuck into his hand.

"Mmm, so are you," Marcus answered, reaching back around Gavin and grabbing a handful of his ass cheek.

Gavin couldn't help but smile. Seeing the hunger in Marcus's eyes made him feel like the sexiest man in the world.

Now, before things got too out of hand...

"Okay, now your back," Gavin ordered, signaling for Marcus to turn around while never taking his eyes off his.

The man was a living canvas—a wall of art covered in tattoos he had collected over the years.

"The neck tattoo, does that mean you spent time in prison?" Gavin asked, wondering if he was crossing some sort of line.

Marcus nodded. "I spent six months in prison when I was in my twenties. Drug-related offenses."

"And what about these? Is there any significance to the tribal tattoos?"

Marcus had tribal tattoos along his chest and arm. As far as Gavin could tell, they were just random designs that ran across his skin.

"No. I just like the way they look."

Gavin continued to wash Marcus's back and under his arms. He had never done anything so intimate before with a man. Usually, his hookups left right after they busted a load. He was lucky if the guy brought him a washcloth for cleanup before pulling up his pants and booking it out the door.

But this right here, washing Marcus's naked body, had Gavin feeling things he'd never thought possible. Yes, he always hoped and dreamed that one day he would find his Prince Charming, but to be standing with him, right this very moment, naked in a shower, had his head reeling.

His hand slid across Marcus's muscular back.

Fuck... Gavin still couldn't believe how fucking sexy

this beefcake was. He admired Marcus's body as he continued to wash every inch.

His back was smooth, but his legs were hairy. There was a tiny bit of fuzz on his butt, just enough to make him look manly, but not enough to confuse him with a wild animal.

The man was perfect.

"Now's your turn," Marcus whispered, reaching for the loofah and dipping it under the water once more.

Gavin's heart began to race as he stood there, naked and hard, staring at the man's handsome face. His jaw was square, covered in a neatly trimmed beard that traced the contours of his face.

Starting with his chest, Marcus licked his lower lip as he began working the suds across Gavin's smooth body. Under his arms, across his shoulders, and down his back, Marcus made a point of working over every inch.

Once Gavin's body was done, Marcus turned him around and slid the loofah between Gavin's ass cheeks.

Gavin let out a moan, surprised and turned on by Marcus's sudden, aggressive handling of his body.

He loved being manhandled.

Gavin leaned his head back when he felt Marcus's warm breath against the side of his neck.

Fuck. Could this man be any sexier?

Taking the loofah from Marcus, Gavin grabbed a handful of suds, then reached behind him, lathering up Marcus's dick.

It was time to take care of his man.

Gripping the base of Marcus's cock, he lined up the head just under his ass.

Marcus let out a growl as his grip on Gavin's waist tightened.

Slowly, Gavin worked his ass back, groaning as Marcus's massive cock slipped between his thighs and just under his ass.

"Fuck... your ass feels so good." Marcus moaned, wrapping his arms around Gavin's torso and pulling him tighter against his rock-hard body.

"Glad you like," Gavin whispered, turning his face up and licking Marcus's bottom lip. "Just so you know, I'm on PrEP, and I tested negative two months ago. Not that I want you to fuck me bare at the moment."

Squeezing his thighs together, Gavin began working Marcus's cock, sliding it in and out of his tight heat, loving the way his length felt sliding just under his balls and between his legs.

"So am I," Marcus whispered, appearing lost in the pleasure he was currently experiencing.

"Fuck... *more*." Gavin gasped, snaking his arm around Marcus's neck, encouraging the tatted gorilla to pump into him harder.

A growl emerged as the beast behind him began to take charge.

Gavin placed his hands on the wall before him,

moaning as the horny stud behind him wasted no time in taking what he wanted.

"Fuck. That's right. Enjoy Daddy's cock. Let me hear how much you need me... shoving my dick between your sexy thighs," Marcus snarled into his ear. "I want to hear how much you love this fuckin' cock."

"Oh yes, Daddy. I love feeling that big fucking dick of yours fucking up into me. Teasing my tight little ass with that throbbing hard cock of yours." Gavin moaned, loving the way Marcus's grip on his body tightened. "Give it to me, Daddy."

These father/son role-plays were fucking hot as hell. Gavin had never been so turned on in his life.

"Fuck yeah. You're such a good boy. Keep working Daddy's dick just like that. I've got a big fucking load for you," Marcus growled, his cock throbbing between Gavin's legs as he pounded into him without mercy.

Jesus. The man knew how to fuck.

"I want you to come in my ass. Mark my hole and make me your own," Gavin heard himself say in the throes of passion. The thought of having Marcus deep inside him, coming inside him, had his dick incredibly hard.

"Fuck yes!" Marcus snarled, pulling his cock out from between Gavin's legs, then shoving it right between his cheeks in one smooth motion.

The act was quick and violent, and everything that Gavin would have expected from the leader of a criminal biker gang.

It was so fucking hot.

Gavin let out a gasp as Marcus's massive dick suddenly penetrated his once-tight hole.

"Holy. Shit!" Gavin moaned, throwing his head back as he gave in to the sudden pleasure and pain that flooded his body.

Gavin wasn't a bottom virgin by any means. He'd taken his fair share of big fucking dicks, but Marcus's... well, his cock was on a whole other level.

"More," Gavin demanded, wishing he'd taken the time to properly stretch himself out, but the primal act of having his ass claimed by the horny beast behind him was every fantasy he'd ever had, come true.

The aggression.

The violence.

The hunger.

It all added to the passionate act they were both sharing. Gavin had never wanted a man so bad.

The stretch of his ass was incredible. Feeling Marcus pound into his ass raw, claiming it, owning it.

Gavin was in heaven.

"*Fuck* yeah! Give me that load!" Gavin shouted, losing all control as he pushed his ass back to meet Marcus's violent thrusts forward.

He was almost there.

Then it happened.

A feral growl emerged from Marcus's mouth as his fingers on Gavin's waist dug deep into his skin.

Marcus continued to slam forward as he emptied his balls into Gavin's tight little hole.

Lights flashed before Gavin's eyes as Marcus's cock rubbed up against his prostate.

Before he knew what was happening, ropes of cum shot from his dick as Marcus's cock milked his prostate.

He had never come hands-free before, but he wasn't surprised that it happened with someone like Marcus. The man was pure testosterone sex appeal.

From his massive muscles to his commanding presence, there wasn't anything about the guy that Gavin didn't find attractive. Even his sweet and thoughtful gestures had him swooning internally.

Marcus's head fell into the crook of Gavin's neck as he inhaled deeply, struggling to catch his breath.

"Fuck. That. Was..." Marcus paused as if he were trying to remember his words. "So hot."

Smiling, Gavin turned his head and captured Marcus's lips in his. They kissed passionately, mouths melding together as their bodies became one.

"So fuckin' hot," Gavin agreed, smiling as he pulled away from his protector.

23

GAVIN

After their shower, Gavin changed into a pair of shorts and a T-shirt, while Marcus threw on a pair of joggers and nothing else—his usual "chill at home" outfit.

"So, what do you want to watch?" Gavin asked, scrolling through the list of movies on the television.

It was a massive seventy-five-inch TV because, of course, nothing about Marcus was small. But who was Gavin to complain?

Marcus was bent over, placing logs into the fireplace just below the television he had mounted on the wall.

"Umm, anything. Just no romance, musicals, or foreign films."

"So, basically nothing with style or taste," Gavin joked, glancing down at the man's beefy man-ass. "You must do a massive amount of squats, man."

Marcus looked over his shoulder at him, confused, before realizing what Gavin was referring to. He glanced down at his ass, then shook his head.

"Stop eye-fucking me, you little perve."

Gavin chuckled.

"It's hard not to, when you've got such a massive booty."

Standing, Marcus lit a match, then tossed it into the fireplace. Like the badass he was, the wood and kindling burst into flames like he was the god of fire or something.

The man hiked up his joggers before stalking toward the sofa.

The guy was the greatest cocktease and totally unaware of his massive superpower. How he was allowed to do anything besides fuck was almost criminal.

Marcus flopped down next to Gavin and let out a breath.

"I know, it's criminal that God made me this sexy, but I swear to you, under all this hot man-beef is just a humble country boy, trying his best to lead a good, wholesome life," Marcus spouted, leaning back on the pillow as if he didn't have a care in the world.

"Wow, that's a load of crap," Gavin said, popping a handful of popcorn into his mouth before offering some to the humble sex god lounging beside him.

"It's true. Ask anyone. I'm humble as shit."

Gavin patted Marcus's lap.

"Sure you are, babe."

Letting out another breath, Marcus lifted his beer to take a sip. “Did you decide what movie we’re going to watch?”

“How about something scary? Could be fun to cuddle up tonight. All alone in this big empty house.”

“My dick is taking a rest. It’s off-limits for the foreseeable future,” Marcus said, taking another sip of beer and settling further into the sofa to get more comfortable for the movie.

“We’ll see about that. You can’t tease a bottom like that and not expect him to devour that cock again with his ass some more. Rest up, stud. Your dick is about to get very chafed in the next few hours.”

He swore he saw Marcus smirk. *Yup, he was definitely breaking through Marcus’s defenses.*

“Okay, back to the horror movie. Which did you pick?”

Gavin hit play and snuggled into Marcus’s side. He was half expecting Marcus to protest, but instead, he wrapped his arm around Gavin’s shoulder and pulled him into his side.

Puppy hopped up onto the sofa and snuggled between both of their feet.

“So, where are your parents in all of this?” Marcus asked as the movie started playing. The question caught Gavin off guard.

He shrugged. “Well, I saw them in the hospital the night I was attacked. They kept lecturing me on how it was my fault. I should never have gone home with someone I just met that night." Gavin fidgeted with the fabric of his shorts. "They basically accused me of being a slut. They didn't seem to care that someone tried to murder me, or that some asshole drugged me and I barely escaped with my life. Yeah, my parents are assholes."

Marcus pulled him closer to his body.

"If it makes you feel better, Ace's and my parents are assholes too."

Gavin leaned up a bit and turned to face Marcus. "Really?"

Marcus nodded, the tattoo on his neck squishing as he moved his head up and down.

"Yeah, they never should have been parents. They acted like kids and only cared about themselves. My dad and Ace's mom spent more time out drinking with their friends and taking off on road trips than they did taking care of either of us."

"I'm sorry, that must have been rough."

"It taught me to grow up real fast. In addition to being Ace's older stepbrother, I was his mother, father, teacher, and protector."

"And now, you're the father for a horde of bikers," Gavin joked, smiling up at Marcus.

"Yeah, I guess you're right. But bottom line, while your parents might be dicks and not be there for you, just know that we're your family now. And we'll always be here for you."

Hearing those words made Gavin's heart swell. All his

life, he'd never felt like a priority in his parents' lives, never being able to grab their attention or spend any sort of meaningful time with either of them.

Yet, here a man was—someone he barely knew—welcoming him into his family, willing to go to war for him, and promising to hunt down and slay the monster who was after him.

Shifting on the sofa, Gavin laid his head down on Marcus's chest and breathed in his scent. The man smelled like sandalwood and hero.

"Thank you, babe," he whispered, wrapping his arms around Marcus's naked torso and watching as the man on the television let out a scream before getting his head chopped off.

What the fuck were they watching?

24

MARCUS

It was just after midnight when the movie finally came to an agonizing conclusion. Normally, Marcus enjoyed horror movies, but this... this one was painful to watch. He wasn't sure whose dick had to get sucked in order for that movie to be made, but whoever it was, Marcus hoped that the man experienced erectile dysfunction for the rest of his life.

"Movies—" Marcus began, before looking down at the sleeping twink nestled comfortably into his chest.

Apparently, Gavin had left him alone to suffer while he escaped to dreamland, no doubt enjoying himself on stage while performing with Beyoncé or Gaga. Or perhaps he was starring in a twelve-man orgy—cocks and balls everywhere, each taking their turn to satisfy the blissed-out little twink.

Marcus wasn't exactly sure what it was that gay men in

their twenties dreamed about, but whatever it was, Gavin sure looked at peace.

Trying his best not to move him, Marcus snaked his arms under the boy, then lifted him so he could carry him to bed.

"Come on, Puppy. Time for bed," Marcus called after the dog, who was nestled up on the area rug by the fire, enjoying his own little midnight snooze.

Puppy stretched himself out before happily following his masters up the stairs and down the hall.

Once they reached the bedroom, Marcus used his back to push open the door, then the moonlight from the bedroom window to guide him to the bed.

Gently, he lowered Gavin onto the plush surface, then removed his socks and T-shirt, before carefully loosening his shorts and sliding them off his body.

Lying there in the moonlight, the boy looked so peaceful and gentle. His pale white skin stood in sharp contrast to the jet-black hair that fell across his face. To say he looked like a sleeping angel did not do the creature before him justice. How did one capture the essence of such beauty?

Look at him, being all poetic and romantic.

Marcus carefully moved some of the fallen hair from Gavin's forehead.

What was he doing?

Staring at the boy... in the dark... while he slept...

'Cause that wasn't crazy serial killer behavior or anything.

Kissing his fingers, Marcus hesitated before gently pressing them to the boy's cheek.

Was it possible that one could be straight their entire life, then meet someone and suddenly change their sexual orientation?

Marcus had never been attracted to men before in the past. Yes, occasionally he found a guy attractive, but he never felt that urge or desire to be intimate with a man.

Fucking around with Gavin in the shower had been so incredibly hot. Marcus was afraid to think about it. Feeling Gavin's body pressed up against his. Feeling the way his body quivered when he shot his load into Gavin's ass... bare. The whole thing had been... unbelievable.

Marcus continued to watch the boy sleep, nestled happily in Marcus's king-size bed, blissfully unaware of the dangers of the world around him.

This was the Gavin that Marcus always hoped he would see—someone relaxed, carefree, and blissfully happy.

Removing his joggers, Marcus folded them, then placed them on the chair in the corner of the room.

"Up," Marcus said to Puppy, who was patiently waiting for Marcus to give him orders.

Puppy hopped onto the bed, then immediately moved to the other side of Gavin, knowing that Marcus liked to snuggle up behind the boy.

Good boy, Marcus thought to himself.

Sliding into bed, he wrapped his body around Gavin, then waited as he shifted in his sleep, snuggling in closer to Marcus before letting out a relaxed sigh when he finally found the spot that made him happy.

Yes, Marcus could get used to this life.

Gently, Marcus rubbed the top of Puppy's head before returning his hand to the soft of Gavin's belly. Holding him close, he had never felt so relaxed.

This was where he was meant to be. This was where he wanted to be.

Closing his eyes, it didn't take him long to drift off to sleep, blissfully unaware of the monster that lurked outside.

25

GAVIN

The room was quiet as Gavin slowly opened his eyes. Light from the moon outside streamed through the bedroom window, casting shadows along the walls that seemed to dance to the silent rhythm of the breeze outside.

Slowly, Gavin rolled over, expecting to find Marcus sound asleep behind him. Instead, he found an empty bed with ruffled sheets, the only evidence that someone had once lain there.

A whine came from Gavin's feet as Puppy looked up at him, as if questioning why he was waking up at ass-crack o'clock.

"Shhh," Gavin whispered to his little bundle of soft fur. "Where's Daddy?"

Puppy turned his head toward the door, as if telling

Gavin exactly where Daddy was—downstairs, somewhere, not next to them in their nice, warm bed.

Pulling the covers off him, Gavin sat on the side of the bed and opened the house's security app on his phone.

Earlier that night, Marcus had downloaded the house's security app to his phone and shown him how to access the security footage of the cottage they were staying in.

"This way, you can always find me whenever I'm not in the same room with you," Marcus had explained to him.

He knew that Marcus was doing everything possible to make him feel as safe and secure as he could. And Gavin loved him for that.

If he was being honest with himself, Gavin loved the feeling he got every time he was standing close to the growly, thoughtful beast of a man.

Scrolling through the video footage in search of his six-foot-four personal bodyguard, he stopped when he came to a shot that showed a set of muscular legs sticking out from under a car.

"There you are." Gavin moaned, grabbing his crotch as his eyes homed in on the massive bulge that appeared on the screen.

Marcus was in the garage, working on a car, in nothing but a pair of underwear.

Licking his lips, a wicked idea began to form in his head.

Closing out of the security app, Gavin opened the

social media app he, Ace, and Lucas had been using to chat.

"Perfect," Gavin said when he noticed Ace's profile was set to green. He decided to message his buddy.

Gavin: Hey buddy, you up?

Ace: Ya. Why? Everything ok?

Gavin: You watching me on the security feeds?

Ace: Yup! Nice Hello Kitty PJs.

Lucas: Gavin has Hello Kitty PJs?? Must have pic now!

Gavin chuckled when he realized he and Ace were not alone in this conversation. It appeared that Lucas was also up at this godforsaken hour.

Gavin: Ace lies. Clearly, he is so exhausted from all that knitting he is doing that he is no longer seeing straight.

Ace: Honey, I haven't seen straight since before I got hair on my balls.

Lucas: Never doubted your queerness, babes. So, what are we all doing up on the party line?

Gavin: Actually, this message is for Ace. You still watching the cottage surveillance cameras?

Ace: Yup! Just as Marco-lini ordered.

Hmm, this wasn't going to do.

Gavin: I need you to stop watching the video feed in the garage for about forty-five... no, make that an hour.

Lucas: Why? What's going on in the garage? Is everything ok?

There was a long pause as Gavin waited for Ace to respond.

Ace: My brother is in the garage fixing that piece of shit car he bought almost two years ago. Why do you care if I see him doing that?

Gavin: Cus he won't be doing that for very long... and I don't think you want to watch what I'm going to make your brother do to me next.

Gavin added a devil-face emoji at the end of his message.

Lucas's next message contained an eggplant emoji, an arrow, and a glazed donut.

Gavin chuckled. Puppy turned to look at him with judgment in his eyes.

Ace: You're right. I don't need to be violently ill for the rest of my life.

That message was followed by a puking emoji face.

Ace: Camera is going down for the next two hours... just to be safe.

Gavin: Two hours?!? Have you seen your brother's package? Two hours and I'll need an ICU! An hour is about all any human can take!

Lucas: LOL

Ace: Arg! We are no longer friends. Good night, my horny ferret.

Gavin: Thanks! Love you bois, too!

With that, Gavin tossed the phone down on the bed and went rummaging through his bags for supplies.

Once he found what he needed, he ran into the en suite bathroom to begin prepping himself. There was no greater mood killer than having to wait for your partner to stretch himself out. And given the size of Marcus's meat and the beating he took only a few hours earlier, he wanted to make sure that his poor ass was good and ready.

When he was finally ready, he left Puppy in the bedroom and crept down the stairs, headed to the garage. No need to traumatize Puppy with his Daddy's midnight activities.

Buzzing with excitement, Gavin opened the door slowly and quietly slid into the double-car garage—because what cottage didn't come with a double-car garage?

Quietly, Gavin tiptoed over to where Marcus was working, completely oblivious to his presence—so much for his ever-alert bodyguard.

How to do this? Gavin wondered, looking around the room for inspiration.

No matter what he did, the moment he made a sound, Marcus was going to hit his head on the underside of the car when startled and alerted to his presence.

Shrugging, Gavin decided that there was no other way.

Removing his underwear so he was completely naked, he glanced up at the security camera and prayed to God that Ace wasn't still watching.

Licking his lips, he stepped up to Marcus and lowered himself down onto Marcus's thighs.

"What the?" Marcus startled, banging his head on the underside of the car as he jerked up, just as Gavin had predicted.

Gavin chuckled. He felt bad but also didn't.

Marcus's body lowered and began to relax once more.

"Oh, it's only you."

Gavin ground his ass into Marcus's crotch, making himself more comfortable.

"Yes, it's only me."

Marcus resumed fixing whatever it was he was fixing, as if Gavin weren't sitting naked on his bulge.

"So whucha doin'?" Gavin asked, slowly rolling his hips back and forth. He could feel the rod beneath him begin to thicken.

"Umm, I couldn't sleep, so I decided to come out here and work on this beauty."

"It's a nice car." The vehicle was red and black and had one of those retractable roofs you could pull back in the summertime. It was a total "fuck me hard in the back seat" kind of car.

Totally badass.

Totally Marcus.

It wasn't exactly the piece of shit that Ace had made it sound like.

"Thanks. It's a 1970 Dodge Challenger. I bought it off... a friend a few years ago. Been restoring it bit by bit ever since."

"So, is that code for you won it in a drug deal?"

Marcus laughed. "I'm not sure you know how drug deals work."

Gavin couldn't help but smile. He continued to grind his ass along Marcus's now very hard dick, enjoying the feel of his mushroom head as it slipped across his hole.

"So, what are you doing up?" Marcus asked, still ignoring the boy currently dry humping his dick.

Fuck, his dick was so nice and hard.

"Oh, I was bored. Thought I'd come out here and play with you for a bit." This time, Gavin reached beneath him and began stroking Marcus's cock.

The man jerked up once again, bumping his head and cursing as he dropped whatever tool it was he was currently holding in his hand.

He suddenly appeared to be in panic mode.

"Ace. Watching," Marcus rushed, trying his best to scramble out from under the car.

Gavin squeezed his legs together, pinning Marcus in place.

"Already taken care of. I told him, unless he wanted to watch his brother get his balls drained, he should probably stop watching the cameras."

Marcus tried to move once again, only giving up when he realized he was totally at Gavin's mercy.

"It's time we stopped playing games. I know you want me, and you know that I want you," Gavin said, pulling Marcus's thick, hard dick out between the folds of his underwear.

Yup, the man was definitely turned on.

"Gavin... we... can't."

"And why is that?" Gavin asked, reaching for the bottle of lube and popping up the cap. "You're on PrEP, right? You already know that I am."

"Yeah... but..." Marcus began, placing his hands on Gavin's thighs, but not really making any effort to pull him off him.

"But nothing." Gavin lubed up Marcus's fingers, then guided them to his hole and pressed them forward. "Lube up my hole, stud. I'm already prepped and ready to go."

It was funny giving Marcus orders, especially when he couldn't see the man's frustrated face, which was still hidden under the car he was fixing.

He heard Marcus let out a gentle exhale before his fingers began working his hole as instructed. For a man who claimed not to have ever had gay sex before, he certainly seemed to know his way around a man's body.

"Ahh, that's right." Gavin moaned, closing his eyes and riding Marcus's fingers as he worked himself open. One could never be too prepared.

After a few minutes, Gavin slid off Marcus's fingers, then grabbed the bottle of lube once again. This time, he applied a generous amount of lube along the length of Marcus's dick.

Fuck, his meat was so big and thick. Marcus was definitely the alpha of the pack.

"Wait," Marcus rushed, using the power of his body to

lift himself and Gavin off the ground as he slid his body out from under the car. He smirked up at Gavin. “I want to see your face as I split that ass of yours in two.”

Gavin couldn’t help but chuckle. The man was such a dude sometimes.

“Whatever,” Gavin responded, trying to act all cool and collected when really, he couldn’t wait to hop on the man’s dick and go for the ride of his life.

Unable to wait any longer, he grabbed the base of Marcus’s cock and lined it up with his eager hole.

Eyes locked together, Gavin began to lower himself down.

“Fuck…” Gavin groaned, closing his eyes as he tried to relax and concentrate on opening his hole and accepting that massive rod that no man alive had any right to possess.

Like, seriously, what were they feeding these Shadow Viper guys?

From what Lucas and Ace had told him, both of their men were also abnormally large. And then there was the Russian. Apparently, that guy was so big that his fiancé was often seen limping around for days after they fucked.

“Breathe,” the voice below him said, bringing his mind back into focus. “Just relax and let Big Daddy inside that tight, little hole.”

Gavin looked down at Marcus and gave him a glare. “I’m trying to relax, but somebody already destroyed my hole a few hours earlier.”

Marcus chuckled. “Fair enough. Want a break?”

Gavin’s eyes narrowed. “Ask me that again, and I’ll cut off your dick while you sleep. Now, shut up and let me ride you. This isn’t the first porn-star dick that I’ve had to take.”

A growl escaped from Marcus as he tightened his grip on Gavin’s hips.

It seemed that someone had a jealous side. That was kind of hot.

Staring into Marcus’s hungry chestnut eyes, Gavin gritted his teeth and forced himself down on the last few inches.

Jesus Christ. His ass never felt so fuckin’ stretched out before in his life.

This was easily the biggest dick he had ever taken, but he wasn’t about to tell the massive gorilla under him that. He wanted to keep the beast on his toes and keep him wondering.

“Fuck, your ass is so tight.” Marcus groaned, staring up at him with hooded eyes.

Smirking, Gavin began to roll his hips. He was in control now, taking what he wanted while making sure that Marcus knew exactly what he had to offer—a nice, tight hole and an ass that knew how to ride dick.

And man, did that dick feel incredible.

The length and the thickness.

The way it filled him up and threatened to tear his ass apart at any given moment.

Gavin fucking loved it.

Placing his hands on Marcus's chest for support, Gavin began riding his dick long and deep.

"More," Marcus moaned, thrusting his hips upward to meet Gavin's downward pumps.

Picking up the pace, Gavin began riding Marcus's cock like there was no tomorrow.

Faster. Harder. Deeper.

He felt every painstaking thrust deep inside him.

"Fuck," Marcus growled, holding Gavin's hips as he began jackhammering his dick into Gavin's tight hole.

Each powerful stroke thrust against that magical spot that always made Gavin see stars.

"Holy fuck!" Gavin shouted, throwing his head back as he moved his hands behind him, gripping Marcus's thighs for balance and support.

He began thrusting his hips in short, quick motions, loving every surge of pleasure that was sent barreling through his body. Each powerful jolt brought him an inch closer to unraveling.

The man fucked like a god. He'd never felt so much pleasure and pain, both at the same time.

"I… I'm…" Gavin attempted before his mind went offline, and another surge of pleasure shot through his body. "Jesus Christ!" Gavin shouted, grabbing hold of his dick and jerking himself furiously.

He was past the point of no return, and he wasn't sure how he was going to contain his orgasm.

Stars flashed before his eyes as the cosmos collided

and his orgasm slammed into him. Hot spurts of cum shot from his dick and painted Marcus's tatted chest.

Beneath him, Marcus let out a growl as his thrusts became long and deep.

"Fuck, that's so hot. I'm... *coming*..." Marcus grunted, grinding his teeth and digging his fingers into Gavin's spasming body.

"Oh yeah! Give me that load, stud!" Gavin shouted as he rode out his orgasm.

Once his orgasm finally ended, Gavin fell forward, collapsing onto Marcus's sweaty chest. He lay there for a moment, breathing heavy just inches from Marcus's mouth.

Staring into his post-nut eyes, Gavin counted down the seconds before Marcus freaked out and threw him across the room.

Marcus didn't seem like the type to attack him, but when dealing with closeted people, one never really quite knew.

Catching Gavin off guard, Marcus pulled his head down and pressed their lips together.

Gavin stared at the big, bad biker—eyes wide open, wondering what was happening.

Was he really kissing the leader of the Shadow Vipers? The hot, burly stud, who carried him over his shoulder, then tossed him into a trunk when springing him from the clink?

No. He was kissing the sweet and sexy man who

cuddled him at night. He bought him a puppy, hoping it might help him overcome his anxiety and sleep better. He was kissing Marcus, the sexiest man he knew.

Chuckling, Marcus slid his tongue against Gavin's lips, slowly prying them open as he happily worked his way in.

"Mmm, I thought you'd be more excited to kiss me," Marcus joked, laughing as he continued to pepper soft kisses on Gavin's shocked lips.

Smiling, Gavin placed his hands on either side of Marcus's face.

"I was just giving you a moment to enjoy my sultry lips before I take charge and show you how a real man kisses." With that, he pounced on Marcus's lips, kissing him deeply and passionately, showing the man just how much he'd been dying to kiss him.

Wrapping his powerful arms around Gavin, Marcus pulled him close into his body.

They spent the next half hour devouring each other's lips. Kissing, licking, caressing, and moaning.

Gavin still couldn't believe that he was making out with Marcus. Not only that, but he was also carrying around his seed.

Rutting up against Marcus, he felt the monster cock beneath him begin to thicken.

God, he couldn't wait to take that dick once again—after a short break and a snack, of course.

26

MARCUS

Marcus's brows furrowed when he realized he wasn't hearing any noise coming from downstairs or the living room.

Considering Gavin and Puppy were supposedly both down there, doing god knows what, Marcus figured he would at least hear some one-sided chatter—because Gavin never stops talking. Unless, of course, he was sticking his dick in said mouth. Then the boy was too busy gagging and tearing up to continue his endless trove of useless chatter.

Even Puppy was being suspiciously quiet. Usually, you could hear the furball panting or whining or chewing on things that he wasn't supposed to chew on.

So, for both of them to be completely silent, Marcus had cause for concern.

Standing in the hallway, he watched as Gavin stared at

his phone with the concentration of a stripper trying to figure out trigonometry. Puppy, on the other hand, was lying on his back, starfishing, as Gavin subconsciously rubbed his belly.

He understood why Puppy was lying so quiet. He was in the throes of passion, accepting belly rubs from his daddy.

But Gavin? Marcus wasn't sure what had grabbed his attention with such concentration and veracity.

"So, what's got you so focused?" Marcus asked, stepping into the living room and sliding onto the couch next to the boy.

Puppy lifted his head momentarily before realizing that getting up to say hi to Daddy number two was not worth the loss of belly rubs. He lowered his head and went back to worshipping the hand that rubbed him.

Gavin looked up at Marcus with a frown on his face.

"You'd think that with a serial killer chasing after your son, you might want to reach out and see how your kid is doing." Gavin turned his phone so Marcus could see his screen. The last message from his parents was from the day Marcus had picked him up.

"Your parents haven't called you or tried to reach out to see how you are doing since?"

Gavin shook his head.

What a bunch of useless bastards. What kind of people don't check in on their son, especially when his life is in danger?

If it were Marcus's kid, he would be under twenty-four

seven surveillance, locked in a tower, with laser beams and dragons guarding the entrance. Marcus would also be locked in that room, protecting his son and making sure he had everything he could possibly need.

But that was Marcus.

He actually gave a shit about family.

Well, most of his family. His parents could go fuck themselves for all he cared.

The last time one of them had reached out to Marcus or even Ace was six months ago to let them know they were cruising around the West Coast.

Like Marcus or Ace even gave a shit anymore.

"Fuck your parents," Marcus said, slapping Gavin hard on the thigh.

Gavin grunted.

"Come on. Get dressed. We are heading out for a bit."

Gavin's eyes lit up.

"Really? But I thought we were under lock and key?"

Marcus shook his head. He pulled out his cell and pressed Call on Ace's number.

"Hey, what are you guys up to?" Marcus asked.

Ace, Blade, and a few of the other guys were staying in a cottage about fifteen minutes away. They were close enough to get to Marcus if, and when, the killer decided to show up, but far enough away that the killer wouldn't spot them while doing recon.

"Any sign of him yet?" Marcus asked, his eye still on Gavin. "No? Okay, cool. Look, Gavin and I are going to head out for a bit. We'll call you guys if we need you. Yup. Okay. Tell Blade I'm going to shoot him in the face if I hear that shit again. Yup. Violence is always the answer."

Jabbing his finger on his phone, he ended the call with his brother, still threatening murder if he so much as touches his husband and lover.

Marcus chuckled.

"So?" Gavin asked, pulling Marcus from his happy thoughts of murdering the man who was sticking it to his little brother.

"Oh. Sorry. Yeah. No sign of *numb nuts*. But don't worry. We have time. He won't attack yet. It'll take him a day or two to scope out the new environment—or at least that's what I would do. And he won't attack in broad daylight. So that means we have until sundown tomorrow at least before we can expect an attack. So for now, we can head out and enjoy some of the town. There's apparently an apple festival going on this weekend that Ace had seen fliers posted about. Thought we could check that out."

"Yes!" Gavin shouted, leaping from the sofa and charging up the stairs to get ready.

Puppy dashed after him, all excited, most likely assuming he would be going wherever it was they were going as well.

Poor Puppy. Sorry to disappoint.

The festival was quite large considering the population of the small town around it.

There were booths selling homemade quilts, crafts, and other knick-knacky things, while food vendors sold every apple-inspired baked good and dish imaginable.

"This influencer crap that you do, why do you do it?" Marcus asked, as they walked through the row of vendors, each trying to sell their greatest apple-infused creation.

Gavin stole a glance at Marcus before shrugging his shoulders and picking up a figurine of a little girl eating an apple. He turned it around in his hand, examining each side, before placing it back down on the table and moving on to the next vendor.

"I don't know. At first, it was a constant need for attention and validation. Somehow, every time a follower messaged me to say how much they enjoyed my post or how much my opinion meant to them, it made me feel seen and valued. Then, over time, my followers somehow became more. It was like, as long as I had their worship and adoration, it didn't matter that my parents had totally forgotten about me and that I didn't seem to matter in their eyes. I know it might sound silly to those who aren't social media friendly, but to me, it fills a gap inside me that I couldn't live without."

Hearing Gavin's sad explanation tore at Marcus's heart. How could one person feel so alone that they turn to faceless profiles and user tags for companionship and validation?

Gavin didn't seem to realize how special he really was and how much he was adored by the people around him. Ace and Lucas, and the rest of the crew, had fallen in love with Gavin the moment he opened his mouth and locked his sensitive eyes on theirs. He was sweet, ballsy, and always ready to help those in need.

Placing his hand on Gavin's shoulder, Marcus gave it a squeeze, then continued walking with him to the next booth.

"I don't think you realize just how special you are. I'll never understand it, but the second you open your mouth or smile at someone, that person seems to instantly fall in love with you."

Gavin turned and smiled up at him.

"Oh, I think that's the sweetest thing you've ever said to me. You know, the same could be said about you, if you didn't get all growly the moment someone looks at you," Gavin noted.

Marcus gave him a smirk. "My growl is part of my sparkling personality."

"And so is helping out the town with renovations and fundraisers, making sure that your drunk customers get home safely at night, and even secretly paying for the Bradshaw kids to go to college through 'scholarships' that don't exist."

Marcus glanced at him sideways. "You heard about all that?"

"Ace told me one night when I was bitching about you."

Marcus shook his head. "Ace is a liar and full of shit. I have a reputation to keep, so I would never do any of that."

Secretly, he loved that Gavin found those things so endearing. While it wasn't a great idea to advertise that a badass biker was secretly doing charity work and helping out his community, he did those things because he cared about those around him. He and Ace struggled while growing up with neglectful parents, so if he could help alleviate some of that stress and worry from others, he was damn well going to.

"Why don't you go grab us a picnic table, and I'll grab us some apple fritters to munch on?" Marcus asked.

"Sure thing," Gavin said, smiling.

Ten minutes later, Marcus was balancing two apple fritters in his hands as he made his way over to where Gavin was waiting for him at a picnic table. Only, Gavin was not alone.

Marcus stopped short, his eyes drawn to the mystery man hovering far too close to Gavin, and the way Gavin's cheeks flushed as the man whispered something into his ear.

Gavin threw his head back and laughed at whatever it was the man had said, before looking over and catching sight of Marcus.

Marcus's eyes narrowed, and he began marching toward the two, each stomp heavier than the last.

"Beat it, ass-wipe," Marcus snarled once he reached the table.

"Umm, excuse me?" the man asked, clearly caught off guard by the sudden hostile invader.

"Leave now, or I'll rip your spine out of your throat," Marcus added, dropping the desserts on the table and taking a step toward the mystery man.

The man looked over at Gavin, clearly wondering whether the man threatening his life was for real.

"Umm, you better go," Gavin said, swallowing hard as he looked up at Marcus.

"No, I'm not leaving you with this crazed psychopath," the man croaked, clearly trying to regain some level of masculinity, even though his balls had clearly retreated into his throat.

Marcus clenched his fists and took another step toward the terrified man.

The man's eyes went wide seconds before he turned and walked away quickly.

"What was that pussy saying to you?" Marcus growled, standing over Gavin, rage and jealousy coursing through his veins.

"Nothing. He came by and told me he thought I was cute and wanted to know if he could buy me a drink," Gavin answered, shrugging his shoulder like it was no big deal.

It really wasn't a big deal. It was just a casual misunderstanding by a man who thought Gavin was single, or here by himself.

Argh, whatever.

Marcus wasn't sure why, but seeing that man flirt with Gavin made him want to commit murder. Take that man behind the shed, bash his face into the wood, over and over, until his nose was in his skull and his body was twitching as his life slipped away.

"What an asshole. I should go and beat his ass," Marcus snarled, turning and ready to hunt down that perverted little shit.

Gavin grabbed his arm.

"What's the big deal? So what if someone found me attractive? It's not like I said yes or took him up on his offer."

"Still. He should know."

"Know what?" Gavin asked, looking at him, all confused.

"That you're mine."

"I'm... what?" Gavin asked, releasing his grip on Marcus's arm.

Marcus glared down at the boy. He wasn't sure why he had said that. The only thing he knew was that he was feeling extremely pissed off that someone was hitting on his...

"Argh!" Marcus growled, not wanting to sit here and process what his heart and brain were trying to tell him.

Instead, he bent down and scooped Gavin up in his arms.

Gavin let out a yelp, clearly caught off guard by Marcus's sudden response.

The next thing he knew, he was tossing Gavin over his shoulder and carrying him back to his motorcycle, caveman-style.

He ignored all the wide eyes and concerned faces as he stomped back to his bike.

"Hey! Put me down!" Gavin protested through giggles and laughs, slapping at his butt as he carried him through the festival and past all the confused spectators.

Smirking, Marcus couldn't help the lightness he felt in his chest. He loved playing with the boy, and if this was what it took to keep his attention, Marcus would gladly carry Gavin over his shoulder for the rest of his life.

He continued to smack Marcus's ass.

"Seriously? If those little love taps are supposed to hurt me in any way, you can save your energy. All I feel is a light breeze tapping against my ass," Marcus mocked as he carried his five-foot-eight, one hundred and sixty pounds of nothingness through the festival and into the dirt parking lot.

"Argh! You're such an—" Gavin started as he hung helplessly upside down.

"Incredible man? Super hot with big muscles and the biggest dick you have ever seen?" Marcus finished, giving the boy a smack on the ass of his own.

"You're impossible."

Marcus couldn't help but smile. He was done fighting against the feelings growing in his chest.

27

MARCUS

Gavin let out a squeal as he threw open the front door, then darted upstairs, almost tripping over an excited puppy bouncing at his feet.

Marcus walked into the home, pulled out his cell, and dialed his brother.

"Don't be watching the indoor cameras for the next... three or four hours." He hung up without so much as a goodbye or waiting for a response.

Smirking, Marcus stalked up toward the primary bedroom, his cock rock solid behind his zipper.

He didn't care anymore if this was appropriate or what others might think. Right now, he wanted to bury his face between those gorgeous ass cheeks, then shove his dick so deep inside them that he could feel the boy's sternum.

"You better be ready by the time I get up there,"

Marcus snarled, pulling off his shirt and tossing it onto the wood floor behind him.

Next, he undid his belt and popped open his jeans, just as he stepped into the bedroom.

Like a good little boy, Gavin lay naked on his stomach, waiting for Daddy to come and take out his vengeance.

"Mmm," Marcus growled. "Now that's the kind of greeting Daddy likes to see from his boy."

"Dinner is served," Gavin said softly, peeking at him from behind bent arms, his blue eyes glinting at him with a dangerously intoxicating charm.

Another growl escaped Marcus.

Stepping out of his jeans, he moved onto the bed and settled himself gently between Gavin's spread thighs.

"You've got such an incredible ass," Marcus snarled, spreading the boy's cheeks so he could admire his smooth hole.

"It's all yours, my horny caveman."

Marcus couldn't help but smile. He liked being compared to a wild beast—one who didn't ask for permission, but took what was his and fought anyone who challenged his claim.

"Hope you're ready to be eaten by a true alpha male," Marcus growled, gripping each of his ass cheeks firmly before diving down between them.

The moan that escaped Gavin was absolutely sinful. If Marcus wasn't already hard, that moan would have sent his dick jamming through the mattress.

He licked Gavin's hole, swirling his tongue and enjoying his new favorite meal.

"More," Gavin moaned, pushing his body back, forcing Marcus to go deeper.

There was something incredibly sexy about eating out Gavin's ass. The desire, the desperation... all of it made Marcus so incredibly hard.

"Oh fuck, right there." Gavin moaned into the mattress. "Jesus, that's good."

"Mmm, you like the way Daddy eats that delicious ass of yours?"

Gavin nodded.

"You're such a good boy. Spreading that ass and letting Daddy have his way with you."

Another moan.

It was clear that Gavin liked to be dominated. He enjoyed taking orders and being manhandled by his alpha.

It was time to give Gavin what he truly desired.

"Top drawer. Lube," Marcus ordered, straightening up but refusing to release his grip on Gavin's ass.

The boy reached into the drawer blindly, then tossed the bottle of lube over his shoulder. It bounced off Marcus's chest, landing next to Gavin's torso.

Marcus chuckled. He loved watching the boy come undone.

Grabbing the bottle, he poured a generous amount of lube on Gavin's hole, then began working it open with one finger before quickly graduating to two.

He wanted to make sure that Gavin was good and prepped. Marcus wasn't exactly snack-sized when it came to taking his dick. He wasn't even entrée-sized.

His dick was porn-sized, and taking all of it required extra preparation and stretches if sex was going to be fun and enjoyable.

And given what Marcus was about to do to the guy, he wanted to make sure that he was stretched and ready. Gavin was going to get every last inch, and Marcus wasn't going to rest until his balls were slapping up against his ass.

Moving from two to three fingers, Marcus watched as Gavin continued to come undone. He moaned and squirmed and gasped out loud.

"Now. I'm ready. I need that fuckin' dick."

Marcus loved the desperation. The need. The hunger. His boy wanted his dick and couldn't wait a second longer!

His dick had never been so hard.

"That's my boy. I'm going to tear that fuckin' ass apart," Marcus growled, the barbarian inside him coming to the surface.

Lubing up his meat, Marcus lined up his cock, then gently pushed forward. He watched as the head of his cock slowly disappeared.

Tight warm heat surrounded his dick. To say that fucking a dude was incredible was no understatement.

The squeeze.

The resistance.

The desperate moan that escaped the poor lad in front of him.

All of it went right to his dick.

"Jesus. Your ass feels amazing." Marcus moaned, watching as his cock disappeared inch by inch.

"Fuck, dude, your dick is so big," Gavin whined, grinding his teeth as he arched his back. "I've never felt so full. So fucking stretched out. Holy fuck."

Chuckling, he began to pump his dick in and out, giving Gavin's ass a chance to adjust to his size.

Part of being a good top was taking care of your bottom... or so he was told.

Unable to hold back any longer, Marcus hoped Gavin was ready.

"Are you ready to take this big, alpha dick?" Marcus asked, stroking the boy's back before giving him a light slap on the ass.

"Yes. Fuck, yes..." Gavin moaned.

"Don't say I didn't warn you," Marcus said with a mischievous smirk.

Tightening his hold on Gavin's hips, he slammed forward, forcing the boy to take every inch of his incredibly thick cock.

He cried out, tightening his grip on the sheets below him.

Marcus smiled. He knew that if Gavin were in true pain, he would ask him to stop.

No. Pain from taking a big dick was always pain that

bottoms happily endured.

"More." Gavin threw his head back and glanced over his shoulder at Marcus.

"You asked for it," Marcus responded, snapping his hips forward again and again.

Watching Gavin's ass jiggle as it slammed against his pelvis over and over was like nothing he had ever witnessed before.

How had he gone this long without giving it to a dude, doggy-style?

Being ridden by Gavin last night had felt incredible, but most of the work had been done by Gavin. Marcus was an alpha, a leader, and the head of a biker gang. He needed to dominate. Take control and fuck without mercy.

He watched his dick disappear in and out of Gavin's ass. He felt the boy's hole tighten, clinging to his shaft like it never wanted to let go.

"More. Harder." Gavin gasped, squirming around as pleasure and pain rolled through his body.

"You're so fucking beautiful," Marcus huffed, sweat dripping from his forehead as he gave it as hard as he possibly could.

At this rate, he was pretty sure that Gavin wouldn't be able to walk for a week.

How bottoms took such a big dick, then lived to tell the tale, was truly amazing.

Marcus was on a mission. He had a reputation to keep, and he needed to prove to Gavin that he was worthy of fucking him. Marcus was in his late thirties, and Gavin was in his mid-twenties. He was the leader of a badass biker gang and a true alpha when it came to fucking.

He was determined to give Gavin the best orgasm of his life.

Picking up the pace, he slapped Gavin's ass once more.

God, he loved his fucking ass.

"Oh! Fuck! Right there!" Gavin shouted, grabbing his dick and giving it a good squeeze.

"Fuck," Marcus huffed. "I'm getting so close." Marcus felt his balls tighten and realized he was about to bust a nut.

"Give it to me, baby. Breed my fucking hole." Gavin moaned, chasing his orgasm as well.

Unable to hold back any longer, Marcus slammed forward, unloading into Gavin.

Feeling Gavin's asshole tighten around his cock, he watched as Gavin shot his load on the mattress below him.

The fact that he could feel Gavin coming around his dick was so fucking hot.

Was this how gay sex felt all the time? 'Cause, if so, he was a huge fuckin' fan.

There was no questioning it. Marcus was now addicted to Gavin's magical hole.

Flopping onto the bed, they turned to face one another. Gavin smiled first, then burst into laughter. Marcus couldn't help but join in. He had no idea what they were laughing at, but seeing the pure joy in Gavin's eyes warmed his heart.

Gavin reached forward and caressed Marcus's face.

"Wow, we are definitely doing that again. Actually, we're going to be doing a lot more of that. Every possible chance we get. Your dick is my new crack. I'm addicted and refuse to kick the habit."

Marcus chuckled at the crazy analogy.

He reached over and pulled Gavin into his body. He pushed the sweaty hair out of Gavin's bright blue eyes before leaning down to kiss the top of his head.

He was dead. Exhausted. Unable to feel his toes, which were currently curled up inside his body.

"Fuck, you're amazing," Marcus whispered, lifting Gavin's chin and leaning in for a passionate kiss.

He grabbed Gavin's ass with his other hand and gave it a firm squeeze.

"I think it's safe to say that I'm addicted to this as well."

Gavin moaned into his mouth as they continued to make out late into the night.

28

GAVIN

"So, what are you doing?" Gavin asked, walking into the living room in sweats and a T-shirt. He walked around the coffee table and picked up one of the books he had been reading.

It was an MM romance about a château in France where wealthy men came to be entertained by high-end escorts. The characters were all flawed and lovable, with an edge-of-your-seat storyline and, of course, a happily-ever-after for each couple.

Marcus looked up from the tablet he was holding and raised an eyebrow at him.

"You're walking funny."

Gavin stopped and glared at Marcus.

"Hmm, I wonder why that is?"

Marcus gave him a smirk.

"Want me to get you an ice pack for your prostate?"

"You're such a gentleman," Gavin answered, sliding into the crook of Marcus's arm and laying his head against Marcus's bare chest.

The man was a tank, with a chest that felt like two firm pillows that wouldn't bend or yield. They might not be the coziest to cuddle, but who in their right mind would turn down the chance to snuggle into the world's sexiest biker?

"So? What are we watching?"

Marcus turned the tablet toward him. Images of Gavin smiling and holding up various products assaulted his eyes.

He was looking at Gavin's social media feed.

Gavin swallowed hard.

He hadn't been on his social media since the night he received those chilling messages from the Valentine Killer.

"I was just checking out your pictures," Marcus said, turning back to scroll through the images.

"Did you check if he reactivated his profile?" Gavin asked, referring to the Valentine Killer. The killer had deactivated his profile the night he'd messaged Gavin.

Marcus shook his head.

"No, it doesn't look like it."

"Good. Hopefully, that means he was hit by a bus and died." Gavin knew he wasn't that lucky.

"So, who are these people?" Marcus asked, pointing to a photo of Gavin drinking at a club with a group of people.

"Just some people I used to work with during the

holiday season. We decided to go out for some drinks one night."

They kept scrolling through the images, with Gavin sharing stories and laughing at some of the stupid poses he had struck. How had he ever thought those poses were cool?

Young and dumb. That had to be it.

Then Marcus flipped to a photo taken about four months ago at a pub for a friend's birthday.

Gavin's heart stopped in his chest.

Sitting a few seats away from the group, his eyes locked on Gavin, was the Valentine Killer.

"What? What is it?" Marcus asked, sensing that something was terribly wrong.

"H-him. It's him," Gavin finally managed, pointing to the man at the bar who was clearly watching Gavin and his friends having a good time.

"Who? The creepy guy checking you out?"

"Yeah. That's him! The Valentine Killer!"

Fear and panic surged through his body.

How long had the Valentine Killer been watching him? Was that the first night?

Gavin grabbed the tablet out of Marcus's hand, then began scrolling through the photos, desperately searching for anyone who even remotely looked like the man who had tried to murder him.

Then he found it.

Another photo. A different day. A different bar.

This time, the killer was standing next to a wall, beer in hand, while he watched Gavin and his friends taking shots at their table.

"Oh my god! He's there as well! How fucking long has he been stalking me?" Gavin jumped up from the sofa and gripped the tablet even harder.

He began pacing around the room, like a scared lion cub suddenly surrounded by a pack of hyenas.

Marcus stood and pulled out his phone.

"So that's the guy? The Valentine Killer?" Marcus asked, snapping a photo of the man on the screen.

Gavin nodded.

Marcus texted the photo to Ace, asking him to scrub the net to see if he could locate anything about the man they were hunting.

Thirty minutes later, Marcus's phone lit up with Ace suddenly calling.

"Did you find him?" Marcus asked, ignoring the sentiment and pleasantries.

"Marcus? Hey, bro. We got a problem," Ace huffed into the phone. It sounded like he'd been running and was struggling to catch his breath.

"What? What is it?" Marcus quickly asked, his stomach suddenly dropping.

"You got about twelve ghosts coming in from the south. They all look armed and are coming in fast. Blade and I are about ten minutes out. The rest of the guys will be there shortly."

The lights to the cottage suddenly cut out.

Gavin screeched, lunging toward Marcus.

"Is it him?"

"No. It's twelve hostiles coming in hot," Marcus growled, grabbing Gavin by the hand and pulling him up the stairs. "Puppy, come!" he shouted. Not that he had to.

As if sensing the danger around them, Puppy was already hot on their heels, chasing after them up the stairs and down the hallway.

Throwing open the bedroom door, Marcus ran to the closet and pulled open the loose board in the back of it. He lifted out a metal box and tossed open the lid.

He pulled out a handgun and shoved a magazine into place with a sharp snap. The sound was ten times louder in the quiet room. Marcus chambered a round, then shoved the gun at Gavin.

"Here, take this," Marcus barked.

Gavin took the gun and stared down at it. The metal was cold in his hands. It was sleek and heavy and reeked of all kinds of danger.

Was this weapon still a virgin? Or had it been used in some sort of crime or murder? Perhaps it was used for protection—scaring off would-be robbers before they even had a chance to enter the home.

Oh, who was he kidding? Any weapon found on Shadow Viper property had a 99.9 percent chance of having been used in some sort of crime.

Next, Marcus lifted a second loose board right next to the first and pulled out an assault rifle.

Gavin's eyes went wide when he spotted the deadly weapon.

"Marcus, what's going on?" His voice cracked as he tried to hide just how terrified he really was.

"I need you to stay in here. Barricade the door and wait for me to return. If anyone gets through that door," Marcus said with a stern, no-bullshit look in his eyes, "shoot whoever it is in the head and then the chest. Then the head again."

"Marcus, I—" Gavin began before being cut off. He'd never held a gun before, let alone shot one.

"I'm going downstairs to protect you and stop whoever is coming after us. The rest of our guys should be here in about ten minutes, so I just need to hold them off until then."

Marus turned his once-soft chestnut eyes toward Gavin. As if sensing Gavin's fear, Marcus reached out and cupped his face.

"I'm not going to let anything happen to you. You trust me, right?"

Gavin nodded. He trusted Marcus with his life, but that didn't mean he wasn't terrified of Marcus getting hurt.

"Watch Puppy for us and keep him safe, okay?" Marcus gave him a half smile. He leaned forward and gently kissed his lips. "I'll be back soon. I promise, babe."

Somehow, hearing those words comforted him. Gavin

reached down and scooped up Puppy from the floor. The poor guy was whining, not knowing what the heck was going on.

"Be careful," Gavin whimpered as Marcus opened the bedroom door.

Marcus shot him a cocky smirk.

"Please, I'm the head of the Shadow Vipers. These pussies don't stand a chance against these guns." Marcus flexed one of his arms, bringing a smile to Gavin's face.

God, he fucking loved this man.

With one last wink, Marcus closed the door behind him. Gavin listened as his footsteps pounded down the hallway, ready to defend him and their Puppy.

How had he gotten so lucky? To have a big, strong man run into danger—battling death, gunfire, and god knows what—all in the name of protecting his scrawny ass.

Taking a breath, Gavin quickly ran to lock the door and began barricading it with whatever furniture he could push in front of it.

They just had to survive the next ten minutes.

29

MARCUS

Standing at the top of the stairs, Marcus adjusted the sight on his rifle as he crouched down, ready and waiting.

He figured his best chance of success was to set up at the top of the stairs; this way, he could see the bedroom, the front door, the living room, and part of the kitchen. It was impossible for him to cover all corners of the cottage, but he figured these were the few strategically important places he needed to defend.

He didn't need to kill them all; he just needed to hold them off until the rest of his crew arrived.

Judging by the sheer number of men coming to attack them, Marcus figured it must be a rival crew seeking revenge or taking advantage of a vulnerable opportunity to take him out.

They must not be aware of the rest of his crew lurking in the shadows and keeping an eye on things.

That only left one question: How did they know that he was out here, alone, in the cottage?

Crouching in the shadows, Marcus waited for his attackers to make the first move.

The cottage was dark except for the tiny slivers of moonlight that streamed in through the open windows. Some might call the lighting romantic. Others, unsettling. To him, it was perfect, offering just enough light to track the shadows while keeping him safely concealed.

A creak on the front porch betrayed someone's position.

Marcus cocked his rifle and fired. The blast tore through the front door, wood exploding outward as the figure beyond it dropped with a painful cry.

"Shit!" someone said from the other side of the door, followed by what sounded like several men scrambling for cover.

Marcus smirked. *That's right. Who's next, motherfuckers?*

He didn't have to wait long.

The window in the living room shattered as two men dressed in black jumped through the window and began shooting in all directions.

Amateurs.

Marcus pumped his rifle once again and fired two shots at the idiots currently murdering his living room.

Both men dropped to the floor, dead from multiple shots to the chest.

Three down. Several more to go.

The next thing he knew, chaos erupted. Glass shattered behind him, then two more windows exploded in the kitchen below. The front door crashed open, while three men rushed the corner, weapons raised and eyes searching for their target.

Whirling around, Marcus opened fire on two men scaling the upstairs windows. One got hit, dropping his assault rifle and clutching his arm.

The second man returned fire, causing Marcus to leap to the other side of the hallway, ducking quickly behind a small table he used as a decoration.

The wood exploded in front of him.

Okay. Perhaps that was not the most intelligent spot to hide.

Marcus dove to the other side of the hall, returning fire at the man trying to murder his bloody ass.

He still couldn't tell which fuckers were trying to kill him. He had a feeling it was the New Mexico Greens. He had humiliated their leader a few weeks ago, so he wouldn't be surprised if this was their boss's way of trying to prove that he actually has balls. But when you are part of the criminal underworld, you never really know who your true enemies are.

Something exploded downstairs. Most likely a result of a grenade that had been thrown.

Man, these guys really meant business. It was almost flattering that it took this many men—and this much firepower—just to try to take him down. Marcus felt his pride flare, his peacock feathers ruffling.

Because Marcus was never one to back down from a fight, he jumped to his feet and began shooting at the men down the hall.

Pain-filled cries and the agonizing sounds of death followed, indicating to Marcus that his targets were no longer threats.

"Marcus! We're here!" Blade shouted from somewhere downstairs.

Something that sounded like metal cutting through air could be heard, which was suddenly silenced by the gut-wrenching sounds of a man who was drowning in his own blood.

Marcus smiled. It sounded like Blade got his target.

"Get your ass down here!" Ace shouted between bursts of rapid fire, followed by shouts and crashes as people fell dead, apparently taking plates and other breakable items with them that Marcus would surely have to clean up once all this bullshit was done.

"Marcus!" Ace shouted again.

"Yes! Coming. Just have to grab Gavin," Marcus shouted down to his brother, dodging a bullet that nearly took off his head. He took off running down the hallway back to his bedroom.

Once Marcus reached the door, he turned the knob, then slammed his body against it to push it open.

The door moved slightly.

What the fuck?

Marcus peeked through the tiny opening.

"Gav. Open up. It's me," Marcus called, twisting his neck as he tried to see around the door and into the bedroom.

Nothing. No answer.

"What the fuck?" Marcus gulped, pushing against the door like he was the Hulk and the door was a piece of paper.

Adrenalin can be powerful.

The door flew open.

Marcus stepped inside and looked around the room.

Nothing.

The room was empty and quiet.

Not even Puppy was found, bouncing around or nipping at his ankles.

Where the fuck was he?

A soft, warm breeze blew across his face, drawing his attention to the large open window.

Did he...?

Marcus ran to the window in a panic and glanced out.

Outside, the attack continued. Men were shooting, and bodies were falling.

They took him! Marcus thought to himself. He glanced

around at the chaos but couldn't see his black head of sunshine anywhere.

His stomach dropped as his mind started racing.

Who knows what kind of sick and twisted things whoever these guys were had planned for the young man he'd spent weeks protecting?

Anger and nausea flooded his system.

One thing was certain: He was going to take his time murdering whoever broke into his house and kidnapped the one man who had taken hold of his heart.

"Marcus!" Ace shouted once again.

More gunfire erupted.

These men were dead.

Running to the closet, Marcus grabbed the second assault rifle he hadn't had a chance to grab earlier.

Eye's narrowing, he ground his teeth. It was time to blow off some fucking heads.

Anger fueling his muscles, Marcus ran into the hallway to take out his revenge.

Forgetting that he was human and not a muscle-clad superhero, Marcus leaped over the banister and landed on the hardwood floor of his living room below.

He had to admit that the move was fucking awesome. Too bad the rest of the guys weren't there to see it. Perhaps he could show them the security feeds later on.

Marcus opened fire, taking out two surprised men, before diving behind the sofa, which was nothing more than shattered wood and floating fabric.

“Marcus, behind you!” Blade shouted from the kitchen doorway as he threw two blades at a man approaching Marcus from the other side of the sofa.

The blades found their mark—one striking the man in the chest, the other his eye. His body convulsed before collapsing to the floor, blood spreading quickly beneath him.

Blade was a killer shot. He’d been trained by the best—his father, who also tried to kill him—and he never missed.

“Nice shot.” Marcus jumped to his feet, then jogged over to where Ace and Blade were waiting.

“Where’s Gavin?” Ace asked, glancing around the room.

“They took him,” Marcus growled, pissed and ready to pull apart some limbs. “Where are the others?”

“Outside, cleaning up the garbage,” Blade answered, walking over to the man lying dead in the living room and pulling his blade free from his eye. He wiped the man’s blood and brain matter on the thigh of his jeans.

He didn’t seem to care that he was now walking around with someone’s DNA and probably last thoughts smeared all over the surface of his leg.

“They couldn’t have gotten far with Gavin. I only left him alone for ten minutes. Let’s go,” Marcus said, rushing toward the front door and leaping over two bodies whose faces were now splattered across the stone walkway.

God. He'd have to pressure wash his home just to wash away the remnants of a failed murder attempt.

Fuck!

Outside, the world around him was at war. Caden, Nikolai, and Jake were crouched behind trees, shooting at men approaching from the east.

Across the yard, Midas drove his fists into a man with brutal force. Blood and spit stained his knuckles as a maddened smile spread across his face. There was no hesitation in him, no restraint. Some men were born for chaos and violence. Midas was one of those men.

To his left, Marcus heard shouting. His head snapped to the side just in time to see a massive stream of fire lighting up much of his front yard.

Men dived for cover, others burst into flames.

"Die, motherfuckers!" Lucas shouted, holding a flamethrower in his hands as he attempted to barbecue every gang member he spotted outside of Marcus's cottage.

"What the fu—" Marcus began before diving to the ground, narrowly missing the stream of fire as it passed by his face.

"Oh, where'd you go?" Lucas shouted. "Why are you running? Thought you big, bad gangsters wanted to come out and play?" Lucas taunted before shooting another stream of fire toward two men cowering behind a large boulder on the front lawn.

One of the men made the unfortunate mistake of

lifting his head too soon to see if the crazy fire-starting twink was still on their assess.

The man lit up like a Christmas tree.

Fire took hold of his head and spread fast, swallowing his chest and legs.

Marcus watched in fascination as the man ran blindly through the yard, screaming as the flames engulfed his body.

"What? Can't take the heat?" Lucas shouted, firing another stream at the second man still cowering behind the boulder. "You bitches think you can come out here and try to murder my friends? I don't fucking think so."

Another stream of fire.

Lucas began walking toward the second man, murder and rage glistening in the flames reflected in his eyes.

Marcus glanced over at Ace, who was still taking cover from Lucas's wild fire attack.

"Okay, I think we need to get that boy some counseling. Clearly, he's got a lot of pent-up anger," Marcus noted.

Ace nodded in agreement.

"We got him! Over here!" Nikolai shouted from somewhere across the property.

Marcus sprang to his feet, hoping to see Gavin's smiling face staring back at him.

Instead, he saw two men, on their knees, hands behind their heads, staring up at Niko and Jake, who were holding them both at gunpoint.

Marcus walked over to the men.

It was just as he'd suspected. This whole attack had been led by Rowan and his crew. A poor man's attempt at revenge.

All this was because he had humiliated the leader of the New Mexico Greens in front of his men. But what other choice did he have? He could have killed the man, he guessed.

Truth be told, at the time, he was too distracted by Gavin coming to live with him to deal with the headache of taking out a crew leader, then dealing with the shit-storm that usually followed.

Showing the man who the true alpha was seemed like the easier option.

"I should have known," Marcus said, staring down at his rival and competition. "Hate to say it, but you failed. You can't even get revenge right. I'm still alive, and my men have kicked your crew's asses."

"Woo-hoo!" Lucas screeched as he chased another man down to the water, a stream of fire scorching the terrified man's ass as he ran for his life.

Marcus tried not to laugh. That boy had issues.

"I might have failed to get my revenge, but *he* didn't," Rowan said with a toothy smile.

Marcus's stomach dropped. "What do you mean?"

"Might want to check on your boyfriend," the man said, chuckling darkly. "Who would have guessed that the big bad Marcus liked to swallow dick?"

Rage taking over, Marcus grabbed Rowan by the shirt

collar and yanked him to his feet. The man went flying upward, like he didn't weigh a thing.

Staring into the man's eyes, Marcus sneered back at him. "What did you do?"

Smirking, Rowan shrugged his shoulders.

"I just kept you busy while that psychopath snatched your boy. Did you know that he's killed over six young men? The Valentine Killer. I believe that's what the newspapers are calling him. Quite frankly, I support the crazy psycho's efforts. That's six fewer faggots in this world to worry about. I was more than happy to lend a hand when he approached me and offered to team up."

"You still failed," Marcus snarled, rage snapping through him as he drove his fist into the man's face.

He continued to beat the man, over and over, blood flying everywhere as Marcus crushed the man's face. It was because of this piece of shit that Gavin's life was now in danger.

The world fell away as Marcus's mind disconnected from his body. All that remained was pure rage and violence.

It wasn't until Ace's voice finally cut through the haze that Marcus realized he was standing over Rowan's crushed skull.

The man was dead.

"We gotta find Gavin," Ace shouted, bringing Marcus back into focus.

"Give me a gun," Marcus snarled, extending his hand toward Jake, who handed him a 9mm.

A stream of red caught Marcus's eye.

Lucas was down by the water, firing his flamethrower like he was trying to burn every mosquito that dared haunt the place.

"Lucas! Stop trying to burn down my cottage and get your ass over here!" Marcus shouted, walking with the guys toward their bikes.

They were about to go hunting, and their prey already had a head start.

30

GAVIN

Stepping away from the bedroom door, Gavin wrapped his arms around himself as he listened to the chaos erupting on the other side of it.

Whoever was after them had finally broken in.

He could hear Marcus taunting them, egging them on, and daring them to step forward and show themselves.

The man had no fear. There was a reason he was their leader. Marcus was tough, smart, and had the biggest set of balls he had ever seen on a man.

Gavin startled as gunfire erupted. Somewhere, on the other side of the door, glass shattered, and objects exploded.

He hoped Marcus was okay.

How much longer until the rest of the guys arrive? Where were Caden and Blade? And Nikolai with that dirty-mouthed straight guy? The one who was married to the ex-stripper with big tits?

He hoped they were close.

But what if they weren't? How were he and Marcus supposed to escape? It wasn't like he knew shit about firing guns. The second he stepped out of the room, he would probably get his head blown off.

Why didn't he ask Marcus to give him shooting lessons?

Puppy began whining at his feet, then began barking like crazy.

Animals were strange.

Gavin bent down and scooped up his little yappy protector. He hoped that having him close to his chest might calm the furry little dude down.

"Shh, it's alright," he murmured. "Daddy number two will be back for us soon. He's just outside, killing all the bad men and making it safe for us to leave this room."

"And who's protecting you from the inside?"

Gavin spun around, his heart jumping at the sound of a deep voice behind him.

Standing next to the en suite bathroom was the monster he'd spent weeks trying to drive from his head.

The Valentine Killer.

Gavin stood there, tightening his grip on Puppy as the dog began to growl at the intruder standing before them.

"Ho-how'd you get in here?" Gavin asked, glancing around the room, hoping to find some sort of escape.

The man nodded toward the bathroom window.

"Too bad your hero didn't think to check the bathroom," the man said, a cruel smile spreading across his face. "Never know when a psycho might be hiding in the shower, just waiting for you to be left alone."

Gavin spun around, reaching for the dresser he had pushed against the bedroom door.

He needed to escape.

"Not so fast," the killer said, lunging forward and wrapping his arms around Gavin.

Puppy yapped and snapped at him, trying to bite off a chunk of his finger.

"You'd better get control of that mutt before I shoot him between the eyes," the man said.

Gavin's mouth fell open as he heard the threat against his baby.

He immediately pulled Puppy in closer, trying to protect him with his body and calm the poor puppy as best he could.

More gunfire erupted behind the door.

"So, who are those guys?" Gavin asked, confused as the Valentine Killer pulled him toward the bedroom window.

"A distraction," the man said with what felt like a smirk. "I tracked down one of your boyfriend's rival crews and handed Marcus to them on a silver platter. The idiots didn't even hesitate."

"You'll never get away with this," Gavin argued, struggling against his kidnapper's pull.

The man snatched Puppy from Gavin's arms.

"How about this? You do exactly as I say, or I snap Puppy's neck?"

Gavin lunged forward, trying to take back his precious little guy.

The man smiled, raising Puppy up above his head. "Oh, now I've got your attention."

Gavin was fucked. There was no way he was going to let this man hurt a hair on Puppy's head.

"We're going out the window. There's a ledge you can step onto, then a wooden trellis you can climb down outside. Honestly, I'm surprised your guy didn't just install an elevator—this place is way too easy to break into."

Gavin clenched his jaw and did as he was ordered. He stepped onto the ledge, then shimmied down the trellis.

He waited at the bottom for his abductor to join him on the ground with his puppy.

As soon as they hit the ground, the killer forced Puppy back into Gavin's hands and shoved them both forward.

"Move."

They headed toward the eastern forest, leaving behind the sounds of war and death. Gavin glanced over his shoulder, wondering if this would be the last time he would ever see Marcus and the rest of the crew. What were the odds of him surviving the Valentine Killer a second time? Nobody was that lucky.

"March!" the man shouted, shoving him hard as he led him through the trees and into the darkness.

Beneath him, the ground was cold and wet. He hadn't

been given a chance to grab his shoes or proper footwear, so his feet sank into the earth below. It wasn't like the Valentine Killer was going to give him a second to quickly run downstairs to grab appropriate footwear.

No. Killers had no regard for comfort or human decency. They got off on pain and suffering, something Gavin was pretty sure he was about to discover.

As they walked deeper into the woods, Gavin held Puppy close to his chest. The poor thing was trembling—no doubt aware of the danger they were walking toward.

"So, did you have fun playing house with that ogre?"

Gavin looked over his shoulder at the man who was leading him toward his death.

"He was a lot more fun than hanging out with you."

The Valentine Killer gave him a smirk. It wasn't a cocky smirk, more of an amused kind of look.

"Oh, trust me. Had you stayed for the rest of our date, you and I would have had sooo much more fun." The man paused. "Well, *I* would have had more fun. You would have been unconscious, totally unaware of the deplorable things that I was doing to you and that sweet little body of yours."

The man licked his lower lip as a wicked smile spread across his face. He reminded Gavin of a snake, staring at its prey seconds before swallowing it whole.

Was this his end?

Had fate finally caught up to him?

Puppy whined in his arms.

"It's okay, Puppy. I won't let the bad man do anything to hurt you," Gavin said as he stroked his fur.

Fifteen minutes later, they came to what could only be described as an abandoned shack.

The windows were broken, with glass scattered across the ledges and the ground. The door, which had no doubt once provided security to the structure, now hung battered and crooked, with the wood barely hanging on to the hinges.

"Inside," the man barked, pushing Gavin forward once again.

This time, Gavin stumbled, falling hands-first into the dirt. Puppy slipped from his hands, landing on the ground with a confused look up at his daddy.

Hunched over on all fours, Gavin stared into the eyes of his beloved pet. He'd only had Puppy for a short while, but the dog had already brought so much joy into his life.

Love, comfort, laughs, and giggles.

Memories of the three of them playing together flashed through his mind. Puppy climbing all over Marcus, licking his face and attacking his socks. Memories of him cuddling Puppy, with Marcus's big, strong arms curled around them both as they slept. Those were good memories. Memories he would always cherish, even if his life was about to come to an end.

Gavin couldn't help but smile.

Those were the memories he wanted at his end.

Puppy gave a whine in the dirt, then stepped forward and licked his nose.

"I know. I love you too. Now go," Gavin whispered, nodding his head to the side, hoping that Puppy would get the hint and run off to save himself.

He had no idea what this psycho was planning on doing with Puppy once he finished having his way with him. But he didn't want to wait and find out.

As if sensing his thoughts, Puppy whined softly and licked his nose one last time. Gavin swallowed hard, giving him a gentle pat before nodding. Puppy hesitated only for a second before turning and running back the way they had come.

"So much for puppy loyalty," the Valentine Killer muttered, reaching down and pulling Gavin to his feet.

At least he knew Puppy would be safe.

Gavin struggled against the man as the Valentine Killer pushed him into the broken-down shack and closed the door behind them.

"There. Now we finally have some private alone time." The man struck a match and lit two of the lanterns that were hanging in the structure.

The so-called shack was basically an oversized hunting shed, one used to store equipment and hunting gear. The room smelled like rotting meat and mildew and something else that Gavin couldn't quite identify.

In the center of the room was a large table—no doubt used to skin animals after their hunt.

A chill ran down Gavin's spine when he spotted the brown and black discoloration on the surface of the table. Years of skinning carcasses and not properly cleaning their surface, no doubt.

Was this the place where he was going to die?

Pain shot through the back of his head as stars danced in front of his eyes.

Gavin stumbled to one knee, caught off guard by whatever it was that had struck him in the back of his head.

Angry hands grabbed him from the floor and dragged his disoriented ass toward the blood-stained table.

Struggling to focus, Gavin was suddenly lifted and dropped on the table like he was nothing more than a sack of potatoes.

Rough grains cut across his wrists as his arms were quickly tied down with some sort of rope Gavin hadn't seen before.

Realizing he was being tied down, Gavin tried to struggle, but his head felt all fuzzy and spacey.

"Shh, shhh, shhh. Don't struggle. You don't want to leave behind such a bruised and broken body, do you? You're so perfect." The Valentine Killer gently caressed the side of Gavin's cheek. "I've been obsessed with you ever since I first spotted your picture online. You were sipping a piña colada by a pool in San Diego. That tiny red Speedo against that perfect tanned skin..." His eyes rolled back in his head. "It was in that moment that I knew I had to have you."

Rough hands dragged across Gavin's skin. He forced himself to stay still, to keep the look of fear off his face, but deep inside, he was screaming, begging for someone to come. He didn't want to die. Not like this. Not alone in a cold, dark shed.

Staring up into the Valentine Killer's cold, dead eyes, he listened and tried to remain strong.

"So, I began to follow you online, learning your habits and becoming obsessed with your life. It wasn't hard to figure out where you liked to go regularly, where you got your morning coffee, where you went to the gym, and even what type of men you found attractive. That was when Robert Ashford was born." The killer leaned forward so their faces were just inches apart. "Out of all the guys I stalked and killed, you were the only one I took the time to get to know. You were my favorite." He gently caressed Gavin's cheek once more. "I had so many plans for you that night after our date. I had a special room set up where I was going to enjoy your body for days and days. I was even going to let the Rohypnol wear off so I could stare into your gorgeous blue eyes as you became aware of me penetrating your body. It was going to be so beautiful."

Gavin turned his head and closed his eyes. The thought of this man on top of him, forcing himself into his body and having his way with him, was more than he could bear.

"Now, thanks to that ogre of yours and his band of merry men, you'll just have to settle for a quick one-time fuck. I had this whole romantic weekend set up. I had rented a cabin not far from here. It was perfect. Secluded, right by the water—the perfect place for me to enjoy your body, then dump your remains once I was done with you. But, once again, my masterful plans got spoiled. I wasn't planning on your caveman boyfriend bringing his entourage of friends, so unfortunately, I can't get us to my escape van without one of them noticing. Sorry, babe. That means that this is our palace of love... and unfortunately, we don't have all weekend to enjoy ourselves."

The man dragged his nose against Gavin's cheek as he inhaled his scent. "You smell so delicious. I wish I had more time to make this evening last forever."

"You're a monster," Gavin whispered, tears sliding down his cheek as he waited.

"Yes. I'm an alpha predator, and you're next on my list."

The Valentine Killer leaned forward and pressed a kiss to Gavin's cheek.

31

MARCUS

Throwing his leg over his bike, Marcus was just about to light her up when he heard the whimpering yelps of Puppy.

Heart pounding in his chest, he got off his bike and watched as Puppy came charging out of the darkness and leaped into his waiting arms.

"Puppy! Where did you come from?" Marcus asked, turning his head away as Puppy peppered him with a million kisses. It was hard not to laugh as he got his face molested.

Pulling the dog away, Marcus scanned the dark, hoping to see Gavin's figure stumbling after him.

Nothing.

No sign of Gavin or anyone else.

"Where did he come from?" Nikolai asked, resting his arms on his bike as he waited for Marcus to answer.

“Not sure,” Marcus answered, still staring at the dark trees ahead of them.

“Gav?” Marcus called, hoping to hear him call back from the forest.

Reacting to the sound of his daddy’s name, Puppy started squirming, fighting his hardest against Marcus’s grasp. The damn dog slipped from his arms and landed on the ground about as gracefully as a drunk ballerina.

Puppy looked up at Marcus, barked, then looked back to the area he had just come from.

“Daddy? Where’s Daddy?” Marcus asked, fully aware that he sounded like the biggest pussy as he spoke to his dog. He could feel the guys watching him from the periphery.

Puppy glanced back at Marcus and gave another bark.

Then suddenly, Puppy pivoted and sprinted back toward the trees.

“I think he wants us to follow him,” Ace shouted, turning away from his bike and dashing after the four-legged creature.

“I think you’re right,” Marcus said, grabbing his gun from the back of his jeans, then running after them.

It’s not every day one sees a pack of bearded bikers running through the woods in the middle of the night. Most bikers stay away from jogging or running, preferring the steady roar of their hog between their legs.

But when it comes to the safety of one of their own, bikers will do whatever it takes to get the job done. Even if that means charging through the woods in the dead of night, searching for a serial killer holding one of their own captive.

Chests heaving and lungs burning, Marcus ignored the pain and focused on the four-legged furball leading them through the darkness.

Finally, the mutt stopped in front of an old hunting cabin. Marcus would have thought it was abandoned—if not for the light shining through the gaps around the crooked front door and the hinges that no longer provided any support.

Puppy plopped his ass down just outside the door and began to whine. He glanced up at Marcus as if to make sure he was still beside him.

Low, muffled voices could be heard from within.

Was this where he had taken Gavin?

Stepping closer toward the door, Marcus peeked between the spaces to get a better look.

Marcus's jaw tightened when he spotted a slimy-looking man huddled over Gavin, caressing his face before leaning down and giving him a kiss.

Oh, fuck no!

Marcus burst through the door, rage consuming every ounce of his soul. Before he knew it, he was standing next to the Valentine Killer, grabbing him by the throat and tossing him across the room.

The man's body flew like gravity did not exist in this part of the world.

Marcus stomped over to the man, grabbed hold of his shirt, and then began beating the man's face.

Blood burst from the killer's nose, as his left eye swelled and began turning a dark shade of purple. The sounds coming from the broken, mangled mess barely sounded human.

It wasn't until Marcus felt someone grab him by his arm that sounds and senses returned to his body.

He could hear yelling coming from behind him. He wasn't sure who it was, but he knew they had interrupted his murderous beating of the monster before him.

The sniveling sack of flesh before him was a dead man. He wasn't going to let a predator such as this walk out of the cabin alive.

"Marcus!"

This time, the owner's voice did cut through the fog in his brain.

Gavin.

His one and only.

Still alive and able to call his name.

Marcus glanced up and locked eyes with the sexiest man he had ever seen.

"Gavin," Marcus breathed out, the name torn from his lips as he rushed over to the table and wrapped the boy in his protective arms. "Are you alright?"

Gavin nodded in his arms. "You came for me."

"Of course I did. I'd move heaven and earth for you."

He kissed the boy's head, then pulled himself back to quickly make sure he was alright.

Once he was satisfied that Gavin was okay, he tilted him back, then took his lips in his.

Joy, relief, love. His body was flooded with a barrage of emotions that he didn't quite know how to deal with.

"God, I fucking love you," Marcus whispered, locking eyes with Gavin and loving the way the boy's face lit up. It was as if Marcus had given him the moon and stars.

"I love you too."

They kissed once again like they were the only two in the room.

It wasn't until someone cleared their throat that they remembered they had an audience.

Marcus adjusted his bulge, then helped Gavin sit up once again.

"What do you want to do with him?" Blade asked, holding a very angry Valentine Killer in a headlock, like it was no big deal.

Marcus picked up his gun and removed the safety.

"Wait!" Gavin said, placing his hand over Marcus's gun. "I've got a better idea."

32

GAVIN

Two days later, they were finally all organized and set up.

Gavin stood in front of Ace, who was holding his tablet out and ready to record.

They were standing in front of a large pit, surrounded by nothing but desert and hills. The area was desolate and unrecognizable. There were no landmarks or structures, nothing that could possibly give away their location to the untrained eye.

That was how they wanted it. They were about to hold a meeting... and sentencing... of sorts.

This was Gavin's masterful plan. It had taken some work to set up and some arguments with Marcus, but in the end, Marcus and the guys agreed with what Gavin was proposing.

"Are you ready?" Ace asked. Gavin didn't answer right

away, his eyes fixed on Marcus as he tried to draw strength and courage from his big, strong protector.

Marcus never lacked courage. He was always so sure of himself. He was a born leader, and everyone knew it.

But this was something Gavin needed to do. This was how he could move on, closing the door on this horrific chapter once and for all. He couldn't be a slave to his nightmares any longer.

"Yes, I'm ready," Gavin finally responded, giving his friend a nod and waiting for Ace to give him the signal that they were live.

Ace raised his fingers, counting down from three. Once the last finger fell, Gavin began to speak.

"Good evening, ladies and gentlemen. You probably don't know who I am, but my name is Gavin, and I am a survivor of the Valentine Killer." Gavin paused, giving his viewers a chance to let that revelation set in.

"I... I almost wasn't though," Gavin said, his voice unsteady. "A few weeks ago, I went on a date with a man who seemed perfect. He was sweet, charming... everything I thought I wanted. And then we went back to his house for a drink."

He swallowed hard, shaking his head as he looked at his interlocked fingers. "He drugged me. I didn't even realize what was happening until it was too late. And then... he attacked me. I don't know how I got away. I just ran."

Gavin looked back up at the tablet, his eyes beginning to tear up.

"I spent weeks hiding, waiting for the police to find the man who attacked me. I kept telling myself it would be over soon, that they'd stop him before he hurt anyone else. Before he found me again."

His voice was rough and shaky.

"But he did. He took me from my home, tied me down in a hunting shed, and... and told me what he was going to do to me before he killed me. I really thought that was it. I thought I was going to die there."

He exhaled. "Thankfully, I was rescued by a band of brave and courageous men. If they hadn't come when they did... I wouldn't be here today. They saved my life.

"So... why have I asked you all to join me on this call here tonight? You are all the mothers and fathers of someone the Valentine Killer took. And I think it's only fair that, together, we decide what happens to him next."

Gavin stepped aside. A floodlight snapped on behind him, washing the area in harsh white light and revealing the Valentine Killer bound to a wooden pole a few feet away.

"This is the man who murdered your sons. The monster who tore your families apart and left nothing but grief behind," Gavin growled, his fists clenched at his side.

Every part of him screamed to rip the man to pieces—to wipe the smugness from his face and make him suffer even a fraction of the pain he'd inflicted on so many others.

"The question before you tonight is simple," Gavin said, his voice low but steady. "Do we turn this man over to the authorities? Let the justice system decide his fate and lock him away in a prison somewhere—assuming that he doesn't get off on some sort of technicality or loophole?"

He paused, staring into the tablet, more focused than ever.

"Or... do we take matters into our own hands and give him the justice so many of us have secretly imagined?"

Gavin glanced toward the bound man before looking back at the screen. "We've decided to put it to a vote. Completely anonymous. No names, no pressure—just your conscience. Each of you can choose what you believe is right."

The man behind him cursed at Gavin. Calling him a slut and a weakling, who had no right to judge him or anyone else in this world.

Ignoring the monster behind him, Gavin glanced over at Marcus, who nodded back at him with his support.

"Before we get started, I wanted to give each of you an opportunity to speak or ask questions. Your faces have all been blacked out, and your voices are disguised by a voice modulator. Your questions and comments are completely anonymous. Now, do we have anyone who would like to speak?"

There was a click on the line as someone played around with their phone.

"Umm, yes. I am victim number three's mother."

"You don't have to identify yourself," Gavin quickly stated.

"No. No. I want to. I want that piece of shit to know how much pain he's caused me and my family."

The woman paused. Her voice cracked as she took a moment to compose herself.

"For the first few weeks after Jacob disappeared, we had no idea what had happened," the woman said, her voice trembling. "There was no phone call. No text. Nothing. He went out one night and just... never came home. At first, we told ourselves it had to be an accident. Maybe his car went off the road. Maybe he'd slid into a lake somewhere. We searched everywhere. We walked the streets, called hospitals, begged for answers. Anything that might tell us what happened to our son."

She paused, sniffled, and blew her nose before continuing.

"Then, the unspeakable happened: The police found his body." Her voice faltered. "And everything broke. Our bright, beautiful boy was gone, taken from us without warning, in the most brutal way imaginable."

She swallowed hard, fighting back tears. "Sometimes, at night, I lie awake and wonder what he was thinking in those last moments of his life. Was he scared? Was he in pain? Was he calling out for his mom?"

Her voice cracked as sobs overtook her. Gavin waited quietly, giving her the space to breathe, knowing every person on the call carried the same kind of loss—the same unbearable emptiness left by the man bound behind him.

After a moment, she spoke again, softer now but filled with something colder. "I can honestly say there hasn't been a single night when I haven't imagined what I'd do if I ever faced the man who took my son from me. And for me… it's simple. Kill the bastard and make it hurt like hell."

Gavin nodded into the camera. He could feel the woman's pain and knew exactly how she felt.

Behind him, the killer laughed and cursed, reveling in their misery as he taunted them with details of the murders he had committed.

Turning his head, Gavin nodded to the man standing next to the Valentine Killer and watched as he—wearing a mask to hide his identity—punched the killer in the gut, causing him to slump forward, gasping for air and ending his tirade.

Gavin said a mental thank you to Nikolai, who was gallantly guarding their prisoner, unbeknownst to the viewers online.

"I-I'm victim number six's father. I say kill the fucker as well. He clearly has no remorse, and why should we allow him to live his life in comfort behind bars when he robbed our children of theirs? Kill the fucker and let us watch!"

Two more parents shared similar sentiments, and it

became clear they needed this moment—a chance to finally voice their anger and seek the closure they had been denied for so long.

"But if we kill him, won't the authorities come after us?" one of the parents finally asked.

Gavin shook his head.

"No. We'll make it look like an accident—a freak death, something natural. Nothing that'll give the authorities a reason to start asking questions. And honestly? I doubt any officer is going to waste time or resources digging into the death of a notorious serial killer. Most of them will just be relieved he's been found and that he's not a threat anymore."

Marcus gave Gavin the signal that they were ready to cast the votes.

"In a moment, you'll be prompted to cast your vote," Gavin said. "You can choose to turn the Valentine Killer over to the police, to be prosecuted under the laws of the United States... or you can choose to let us—the victims—pass judgment ourselves." His jaw tightened, and his voice hardened. "And decide whether this monster lives or dies."

This was it—the moment that would decide everything. The choice that would define what they became after tonight. Would they carry the weight of murder for the rest of their lives, or hand the burden over to the authorities and trust that justice, somehow, would be enough?

Gavin kept his expression neutral, but deep down, he

already knew what he wanted. He hoped that the group would vote to end the monster's life.

Lifting his phone, Gavin cast his vote as well.

They all watched on the live feed as the votes for "Kill Him" continued to rise. Once the final vote was cast, it was unanimous. Every person on the call had voted to end the Valentine Killer's life.

"The votes are in. Now, for those of you who do not wish to witness this execution, feel free to log off this video feed. For those who choose to stay, please note that the death you are about to witness will be violent and brutal."

Gavin nodded at Marcus and his crew, who all began placing wool masks over their faces. Since the feed was live, they didn't want any of the people watching to be able to identify them. They even wore long-sleeved shirts to hide any identifiable tattoos or body piercings.

The only one who was not wearing a mask was Gavin. He thought it was important not to hide his identity. He wanted to connect with the families of the victims so they could see him as he was. A victim. A person. A son.

Once everyone was covered, they all walked over to where the Valentine Killer was tied, seething and cursing, letting his final words fly free.

"This won't change anything! I took them all from you!" he shouted, spit flying from his mouth as he cursed them all.

Gavin looked down into the pit and smiled. Four hungry mountain lions stalked around in circles, agitated, calling to one another as if sensing that dinner was about to be served.

It had taken Marcus and the guys about three hours to lure all four cougars into the deep pit. There had been a few close calls, but Nikolai was surprisingly good at handling wild animals.

Considering the animals' incredible jumping abilities, they had to find a pit that was deep enough to prevent the cougars from escaping before they were ready. Thankfully, Ace was great with computers.

Ace panned his tablet over the pit, showing their viewers exactly what was about to befall the monster before them.

"As I said earlier, when the police find what's left of the body, they will just assume that he had been chased by a pack of hungry cougars and fell into the pit below before being eaten alive." Gavin turned to face the man who had tried to murder him—twice. "I know it's usually you who leaves valentines in your victims' pockets," he continued, his voice steady despite the storm brewing inside him. "But since I'm the one ending this... I thought it was only fitting that I give you one of my own."

Gavin hadn't told Marcus what he planned to do if the vote went their way. He glanced over at Marcus, who stood close to Clive—his face hidden by a thick layer of fabric, but his eyes were visible. And there it was. Love. Concern. Fear. Fear for what this act might cost Gavin.

But this had to be done. This was what he needed to get closure. This was what they all needed.

Pulling the crumpled-up valentine from his back pocket, Gavin unfolded it and glared down at the words that had taken him hours to write.

With the sound of hungry cougars echoing behind him, Gavin began to read his final words to the man who had brought him so much fear.

"To the monster of my nightmares,

You've plagued my thoughts and dreams for the very last time. I used to lie awake at night, too afraid to close my eyes, for fear of seeing your murderous face glaring down at me, as you tried to choke the life out of my body.

But not anymore. Now, I'll be able to close my eyes at night and sleep soundly next to the man I love, knowing that you can no longer harm me. You can no longer hunt or rape or murder anyone else, ever again.

Tonight, I stand for myself and for all those you destroyed—and I'll watch without mercy as the beasts below tear you apart. Just as you have torn apart so many lives.

It will give me great pleasure to listen to you scream in pain and beg for mercy, right up until that very last breath.

So, on behalf of all those you have hurt, I sentence you to die."

With that final word, Gavin took a step away from the pit and nodded to the two masked men standing next to the Valentine Killer. They untied him and dragged him over to where Marcus was waiting.

"Is it my turn now to have a bit of fun?" Marcus asked, his identity still hidden under the mask.

The only reason Marcus had agreed to this video trial was the promise that once the sentence was passed, he could have full range to beat the living piss out of the man. It was Marcus's way of getting justice for all the pain and suffering inflicted on the man he loved.

Gavin found the request so romantic. He never imagined anyone would love him so much that they would demand to take their vengeance on the man of his nightmares.

Smiling, Gavin nodded.

"Good," Marcus grunted, grabbing the man by the throat and pulling him close to his face. "You tried to rape and murder the man I love. Monsters like you don't deserve a quick death."

With that, Marcus punched the Valentine Killer hard in his stomach. He fell over in pain, gasping for air.

"Fuck you!" the man shouted, struggling to stand on his feet.

Marcus kicked him in the face, sending the man flying backward and landing hard in the dirt close to the pit.

"You fucking killed them! All of them!" Marcus growled, lunging at him and landing on his body. He straddled his thighs, then began punching the killer in the face without mercy.

Blood burst from his nose, while sounds of pain mixed with agony spilled from his mouth.

"Please... stop... I'm..." he pleaded as Marcus continued his brutal assault on the man who had murdered so many.

Watching the anger and violence spill from Marcus was intoxicating. Seeing each powerful blow be delivered —all in the name of vengeance for the man he loved—was probably the most romantic thing that anyone could ever do.

This right here was better than being carried off body-guard-style by the man of his dreams.

There was no doubt in his mind that Marcis really loved him.

Wanting to make sure that the man's execution was carried out as promised, Gavin decided that it was time.

"That's enough," Gavin called out, not wanting to use Marcus's name during the live stream.

Marcus grunted, then pulled the battered and beaten man up.

Clive teetered on his feet.

"Rot in hell, you piece of shit." With that, Marcus pushed the man into the pit.

The group rushed forward, gathering at the edge of the pit to watch the remainder of the execution.

Gavin stepped up next to Marcus and slipped his hand into his. Leaning his head against the angry biker's shoulder, he looked down into the pit and smiled—not with joy, but with the quiet satisfaction of knowing it was finally almost over.

They watched as the cougars began stalking their

prey. They circled the man, growling and swiping their paws at Clive's body. The man turned in circles, watching the hungry beasts as they continued to move toward him.

"Please! Let me up! You can't do this!" the Valentine Killer shouted.

The fear spilling from the man made Gavin smile. Perhaps now, the Valentine Killer would know the fear and torment Gavin felt, wondering if or when the killer might find him.

Countless sleepless nights. Tossing and turning. Not being able to close his eyes for fear of seeing Clive's face staring back at him.

That was the fear Gavin wanted his monster to experience.

But there was no mercy to be had. This man had extinguished so many lives in the most unimaginable way possible. The horror and pain that he caused deserved such a violent sense of justice.

"Please! I beg you! Don't let me die down here like this."

Anger shot through Gavin. His eyes blazed with fury as he stared down into the pit.

"Just like you let all those poor, innocent men get violated? Then murdered? Alone?" Gavin shouted down at the terrified man. "At least for you, you won't be alone when you die," Gavin said with a coldness to his voice. "You have all of us here to watch you."

Clive looked up at Gavin one last time. The look in his eyes was one that Gavin would never forget.

Regret.

It happened so quickly. Two cougars lunged forward, attacking the top half of the man as he screamed. Seconds later, the other two attacked, greedily tearing away limbs that they coveted for themselves.

Standing next to the edge of the pit, Marcus wrapped his arm around Gavin's shoulders and kissed the top of his head. It was such a simple and loving gesture.

Marcus would always be his protector, but he was also so much more. He was his love, his best friend, the man he turned to when he was feeling scared or lonely. He was a giant, scary biker with a hidden heart of gold. The love that Marcus had for him and his crew was one of the reasons that Gavin had fallen so hard so quickly. Kindness and love like that were rare in this world.

Standing next to each other, they both watched as the monster of Gavin's dreams was devoured by the monsters of the mountains.

Most would have looked away in disgust. But Gavin and Marcus didn't. They stood side by side, watching with cold contempt as justice unfolded for the victims who would never have the chance to claim it themselves.

One by one, the parents of the victims began to log off. They had finally been given the closure and justice they had always longed for, and Gavin found himself grateful that he was able to give them that.

"Thank you for this," Gavin whispered, looking up into those gentle brown eyes.

"Anything for you," Marcus responded, giving him a kiss on the forehead, even though he was still wearing his mask.

His nightmare was over, and he now had a knight in shining armor to protect him against any future threats.

33

GAVIN

Scary. And awkward as fuck.

That's what they must all look like, crammed into the first two rows on the left-hand side of the stage. A bunch of grown-ass, tattooed bikers, all dressed in leather, some with beards that looked like they hadn't been trimmed in weeks.

Oh, and one ex-stripper turned bartender, squeezed in among them, whose top was doing little more than barely covering her nipples.

Gavin was aware of the looks. Some came from concerned parents, quietly wondering why a bunch of leather-clad bikers were in attendance at a children's dance performance.

Others recognized them immediately and knew exactly who the Shadow Vipers were. They were well aware that one of their members—Lucas—was the director of the class and was currently dating one of the bikers sitting in the front row—the one gleaming with pride and never taking his eyes off the cheery brunette smiling back at him.

The theater was packed, every seat filled with parents and children of all ages, their laughter and smiles carrying through the room as the performance unfolded.

Gavin had to admit, the show was fucking awesome. He'd never been to a children's performance, but seeing the level of enthusiasm and excitement in each of the kids' eyes was something he knew he would never forget.

To have a job like Lucas's, one so impactful and important, must be so satisfying at the end of each day.

Given everything he had been through recently, Gavin was beginning to realize that he wanted to do more with his life. Something that actually meant something to him. Maybe a job where he was able to help survivors of violent crimes cope with their trauma and find a way forward, like he was learning to do himself.

He didn't know exactly what that would look like yet, but for the first time, he found himself looking forward to figuring it out. One thing was certain though—being a social media influencer was not what he wanted to do anymore.

Once the performance was over, they all spilled out onto the streets to take the party back to their bar. This was Lucas's night, and all the Shadow Vipers were there to support him—their brother.

Just like all of them had been there for him to keep him safe and help put an end to the Valentine Killer, Gavin had come to realize that the Shadow Vipers were now his family too. While his birth parents might be too busy and self-absorbed to give a shit about him and how he is doing, Gavin had come to realize that true family was those who showed up for you.

Like Marcus. And Ace and Lucas, and all the members of the Shadow Vipers.

That was family. That was love.

"What's on your mind?" Marcus asked, holding Gavin's hand as they waited with the others for Lucas to wrap things up inside the theater.

Smiling up at the man who had once locked him in a trunk and carried him over his shoulder countless times, he couldn't help but feel his heart expand in his chest.

"Nothing. I was just thinking about how much this feels like family. You, Ace, Lucas, the guys... everyone here tonight, showing up and supporting each other. It's more than I ever thought I'd have."

Marcus wrapped his arm around Gavin's shoulders and pulled him into his body.

"What can I say? Once you're in with the crew, you're stuck with us, babe." Marcus let out a chuckle.

"It's not a bad place to be stuck."

"Nope. No, it's not," Marcus replied, squeezing him tight against his side.

"Evening, gents," Sheriff Burke said as he pushed through

the crowd toward them. A few lingering parents turned to watch, curiosity already sparking. Nothing fueled small-town rumors faster than a sheriff showing up unannounced.

"Evenin', Burke," Marcus responded, extending his hand and giving the sheriff a firm shake.

"Got some great news for you all. We found the Valentine Killer... or what's left of him anyway."

Gavin and Marcus exchanged glances.

"Oh, you did?" Gavin asked, trying his best to remain surprised by the revelation.

"Yup. We found him in a pit some five days ago. It took us that long to ID the body and then try to figure out what happened to him." The sheriff glared at them both before continuing. "Looks like he took a stumble in at some point. Not sure why he was out there at all. Anyway, it looks like some pumas or somethin' done went and ate his ass and shit." The sheriff shook his head. "The scene was gruesome. Blood and body parts everywhere," he explained, switching his gaze between him and Marcus.

Marcus shook his head, his eyes locked on the sheriff. "Damn, that's terrible. The poor animals. A man like that couldn't have tasted too good, in my opinion."

The corner of Burke's mouth lifted in a half smile as he struggled not to laugh and keep his composure.

"Yeah, well, you boys don't know anything about it, do ya?"

Marcus and Gavin looked at each other and shook

their heads. Behind Burke, the rest of the crew stood, watching with curiosity.

"Now, why would we know anything about a serial killer being devoured by four mountain lions in the middle of the night, Sheriff Burke?" Marcus said, letting that very specific detail regarding the number of mountain lions slip, knowing that the sheriff would catch on to the reality of what he was saying.

He and the sheriff had always been honest with one another. This was how their relationship worked.

"Seriously, man. That sounds like something that only happens in movies."

The sheriff nodded, clearly understanding the meaning of Marcus's words. "Sorry, boys. I had to ask." He adjusted his hat. "If you ask me, it sounds like the asshole got what he deserved."

Gavin nodded in agreement.

"Well, I just stopped by to tell you that the fucker is dead, so it's safe for you to go home now, Gavin. Thanks, Marcus, for taking care of this young man and for taking care of... well, for keeping us all safe in this town that we all love."

Sheriff Burke extended his hand to Marcus once again before turning and making his way back through the crowd.

A quiet sense of victory settled over Gavin as he realized the threat of being caught was no longer hanging over them. They could finally move forward, knowing the world was just a little bit safer.

“By the way, you’re not going anywhere, my little spitfire,” Marcus growled, wrapping his arm around Gavin’s shoulders and pulling him firmly against him.

There was no other place that Gavin would rather be.

It was in that moment that the guys began hollering and cheering. A red-faced Lucas stepped out of the theater and raised his hands to calm the ruckus.

He laughed and covered his face as he stepped forward into the crowd. Lucas’s boyfriend, Caden, followed, holding a bouquet of purple roses before passing them to his blushing man.

Lucas took the flowers, then wrapped his arm around him, hugging Caden and thanking him for being such a wonderful man.

Gavin smiled at the two lovebirds as he clapped. He knew how hard Lucas had worked on this show, teaching the kids how to dance while raising money for next year’s program.

Lucas was such a good man. Loving and caring, just like the rest of the guys—and girls—who were part of Marcus’s crew.

Wanting to do something nice, Gavin had secretly donated two thousand dollars through Lucas’s website. He hoped his donation might help his friend get closer to achieving his goal. Over the past few weeks, they had all grown closer as friends. They had all risked their lives to protect him, and Gavin was never going to forget that.

"You did an amazing job in there tonight," Gavin said, leaning in and hugging his friend.

"Thanks! I can't believe how well the kids did. They looked like they were having the time of their lives. And the two who fell and then started fighting with each other? I almost peed myself laughing," Lucas said, his grin nearly splitting his face in two.

"Did you see how packed the theater was?" Ace asked, stepping up next to Lucas and throwing his arm over his shoulder.

"Yeah! I still can't believe how many people showed up," Lucas said. "Sharon told me they actually had to turn people away at the door but promised that next time we're adding a second performance. And the online donations were incredible—we raised enough funds to cover the program for the next two years!"

"Wow, that's incredible! I'm so proud of you, little man," Marcus said, reaching out to pull Lucas into a hug. "Now, let's head over to the bar and celebrate properly."

The guys all cheered, turning and heading down the street to get shit-faced and pass out god knows where.

Gavin was about to follow when Marcus grabbed him by the arm and tugged him back toward him.

"Thought we could hang back a bit and have a little alone time before we join the others to celebrate," Marcus whispered, bending down and kissing Gavin's neck passionately.

Fuck, the man was an animal.

Gavin's cock hardened instantly, every nerve on fire, as he tried to control himself long enough to find a private spot for them to have some fun.

But Marcus had other plans.

Reaching down, Marcus scooped Gavin up and tossed him over his shoulder like he had done the first time they met all those weeks ago.

"Hey!" Gavin shouted, laughing and beating his fists against his caveman's back. "I never consented to this!" Gavin chuckled, pretending that Marcus was carrying him away against his will.

Who was he kidding? Gavin couldn't get enough of Marcus's big, fat dick. He needed it in his mouth, on his face, in his hands, and definitely buried deep in his ass.

"Fuck, I love it when you manhandle me."

A feral snarl erupted below him.

God, he loved it when his man was all untamed and aggressive.

Marcus gave him a hard slap on the ass.

"Fuck, I love it when you do that." Gavin moaned. His eyes were heated, and he was desperately hard.

Moving quickly, Marcus carried him across the town square and up the city hall clock tower.

How Marcus got access? Gavin didn't want to know.

Placing him gently on his feet, Marcus turned Gavin so

he was staring out at the town through the large glass window of the clock.

"Wow, I've never seen such an incredible view." Gavin gasped, taking a step forward and gazing out at the town.

It was well past nine, so the town was dark and quiet. All the rowdy patrons had either gone home for the night or were headed over to Ride 'em Hard to drink till their faces went numb or they passed out from alcohol poisoning.

Gavin gazed at the quiet town, his lips parting as he admired the delicate glow of the twinkle lights illuminating the streets and shops below.

Say what you will about small towns, but their residents take great pride in their beauty.

"This is probably my favorite view of the town. I come here late at night sometimes, just to look out and take in the peace and quiet. It calms me and reminds me why I love this town and the people in it." Marcus wrapped his arms around Gavin's body, then began kissing Gavin's neck. "God, I love you. I want you to stay. Stay here with me. Now and forever."

Hearing the love and need in Marcus's voice was all Gavin needed to be sure of how he felt—how he had always felt.

Turning his head to the side so he could gaze into Marcus's warm chestnut eyes, he smiled.

"There's no place that I'd rather be, big guy. I love you

too much to ever walk away. You're stuck with me now; I hate to tell you."

Marcus began to chuckle, then leaned in and took his lips in his.

There was no doubt in Gavin's mind that he had finally found the man of his dreams. The man who would always be there for him—to protect him from his nightmares and help support him with his dreams. Marcus was the type of man who would walk through fire to get to him.

That was the kind of love and devotion this man was offering. Gavin couldn't believe how lucky he was to find him.

After kissing Marcus long and deep, they placed their foreheads together and breathed in each other's scents.

"We should probably get back to the party," Gavin whispered, reluctantly pulling his lips away.

"Not quite yet," Marcus snarled in one of his deep, feral, hungry voices that always drove Gavin wild.

Pushing him up against the window, Marcus yanked down Gavin's pants and underwear in one smooth motion.

A satisfied growl emerged from Marcus's lips as he dropped down to his knees, then pulled Gavin's ass cheeks apart.

"Fuck... *yes...*" Gavin moaned, leaning forward and giving his man greater access to his ass.

"Fuck, your ass is gorgeous." Marcus groaned before diving in and attacking his hole.

He licked and kissed and shoved his tongue in as far as it would go. Gavin closed his eyes as he gave in to the pleasure of Marcus's magical tongue and hungry mouth. Gavin never felt so sexy and desired. Staring up at the stars, he lost himself.

Somewhere between the moans and gasps of pleasure, Gavin heard the familiar sound of a bottle cap being opened, followed by the cool feel of wetness being rubbed all around his hole.

"Mmm, yes, babe. Work me open so I can take that big, fat cock of yours," Gavin whimpered, pressing back on Marcus's two fingers, hoping he could speed along the stretching process.

He *needed* Marcus's dick, and he *needed* it right fucking *now*!

After what felt like an eternity of torture, he felt Marcus's fingers slip from his body. The sudden absence of Marcus's touch left Gavin breathless, yearning for that intimate closeness once again.

How had he fallen for a man so hard, so fast?

Behind him, Marcus stood, grabbing the lube and lathering up his cock.

His warrior was preparing for battle.

"Are you ready for all this cock, boy?" Marcus was back to his father/son role-play.

Gavin's cock immediately twitched. There was something extremely hot about an older, more powerful man having his way with his younger lover. Marcus's untamed, aggressive nature was such a huge fucking turn-on that Gavin could barely contain himself.

"Fuck, yes, Daddy. I want you to fuck me without mercy."

Marcus's grip tightened on Gavin's waist. Clearly, he liked being given permission to destroy his tight hole.

"You asked for it," Marcus snarled, sliding his cock between Gavin's cheeks and lining the head up with his hole.

Smiling, Gavin arched his back and braced himself for the fucking of a lifetime.

"You ready?" Marcus asked one final time.

"Yes, Daddy. Do your fuckin' worst."

With that, Marcus thrust his hips forward, sending Gavin's head flying back in a wondrous roar of pleasure and pain. Pleasure at having the world's sexiest man deep inside him, and pain at having what felt like the world's largest cock thrust up into his throat.

Those feelings of fullness and connection rolled over him once again. The way Marcus slid his hands up Gavin's body. Wrapping his arms around him. Feeling him. Worshipping him.

This was what he wanted—to have a sweet, powerful, and dangerous man loving him and protecting him. Always.

"Jesus," Gavin groaned. "Your dick is so fucking big."

He could almost feel Marcus's smile behind him.

Cocky bastard.

But he had every right to be cocky. God had blessed him with a big fucking dick, a tool he could use to exert his dominance over others.

To show people what a true alpha was.

And Marcus was all his.

He felt Marcus kiss the top of his shoulder.

They were still wearing clothes. Well, Marcus was. Marcus's dick was out, with his underwear tucked underneath his cock. His balls were probably squished somewhere between his cock and the elastic band of his underwear. But there was something hot and extremely sexy about a man so fucking horny for him that he couldn't waste even a minute to rip off his clothing before jamming his dick into his ass.

Gavin loved it. He felt so *friggin* special.

He, on the other hand, had his pants and underwear torn off—a victim of their pre-fuck, ass-eating adventure.

"It's all yours, baby. Yours and only yours," Marcus whispered in his ears as he slid his hands down to Gavin's hips.

"Give it to me," Gavin whispered, turning his head to the side to give Marcus one final kiss before giving him his body.

With a simple growl, Marcus's hips snapped forward, sending jolts of pleasure flying through Gavin's body.

That was the last thing Gavin remembered.

The assault on his ass was quick and violent. Long, deep thrusts, followed by short, quick ones.

Pleasure.

Pain.

Heat bursting through his body.

Gavin gasped and moaned, completely at the mercy of the caveman standing behind him.

"Fuck, you feel so good," Marcus huffed, slamming into him hard and biting down on his neck.

"More. Harder," Gavin cried out, fighting against the waves of pleasure that threatened to knock him out every time Marcus's cock pressed up against his prostate.

The man was a fucking god!

He wasn't sure how much more his ass, or his soul, could fucking take.

Marcus's grip on Gavin tightened. He was pretty sure he was going to be bruised tomorrow.

"Fuck... Babe... I'm gonna come!" Marcus snarled, giving him one final thrust before unloading inside his body.

Knowing that Marcus had just busted his load inside his ass sent Gavin flying over the edge. With his ass still full of dick, Gavin pointed his cock and shot his load all over the wall.

Tired, sweaty, and gasping for air, they both collapsed into a tangled heap of limbs and lay there.

They both stared at each other, neither one of them looking away.

"God, I love you," Marcus whispered, his eyes never leaving Gavin's.

"I love you too, you sexy brute," Gavin responded with a smile of his own.

They both laughed and continued to stare at each other.

Somehow, in all this darkness, Gavin had finally found his knight in shining armor.

It appeared that romantics do get their happily ever after, after all.

Sometimes it might just take a serial killer and a drive in a trunk to get you there.

34

MARCUS

One Year Later

"You know, sometimes I wonder about that dog. He doesn't seem to be altogether... *there* sometimes," Marcus said, watching Puppy as he rolled around in their yard.

Puppy... yes, they decided to keep the name Puppy after all—confusing as shit as it may be, but Gavin grew attached to the name, and Marcus had quickly learned that whatever Gavin wants, Gavin fucking gets.

Puppy would be running around the backyard, then he would stumble, fall, and roll onto his back. Then he'd spread his doggy arms and legs wide, as if letting the sun warm his nuts, before turning back onto his stomach and repeating the whole course all over again.

At Marcus's last count, this was his fourth time warming his nuts.

"Well, which one of us isn't altogether there?" Ace asked, turning his head toward Lucas, his best friend and part-time psycho.

Lucas nudged Ace with his foot before taking another sip of his sangria.

It was summer, and Marcus was having one of his summertime barbecues at his place—well, now that the little monster had moved in, he guessed it was technically both of their places. Either way, the whole Shadow Viper crew had shown up for the event.

They had just finished chowing down on some delicious steaks and sausages—plant-based "burgers," if you can call them that, for Gavin—and were now enjoying a few drinks out in the sun.

"Well, he did save my ass by leading you to that murder cabin before that psychopath could have his way with me and carve up my beautiful skin," Gavin added.

Marcus reached over and took Gavin's hand. He hated thinking about how close he had actually come to losing his love forever. "Yeah, I guess you have a point. But still. Look at him."

Puppy was rolling onto his back and spreading his legs once again up at the sun. His tongue hung lazily out the side of his mouth, and he seemed to be happier than a pig rolling around in shit.

Gavin gave a chuckle. He stood up from his chair, then walked over to where his beloved dog was staring at him from the side of his eye.

"Oh, don't listen to Daddy number two," Gavin said as he reached down and scooped up his dog. He nuzzled his face into his fur before walking with him back to his seat next to Marcus. "He's just jealous that he isn't as flexible as you and can't lick his own balls."

The guys around them began to chuckle.

God, he loved the sense of humor in his boy.

He placed his hand on Gavin's thigh and gave it a gentle squeeze. "Now, why would I ever need to lick my own balls? That's what I have you for, sweety."

Gavin's mouth dropped open in mock offense. He punched Marcus in the arm, appearing to regret it immediately. Marcus was a solid wall of muscle, so the only thing he accomplished was practically breaking his hand on Marcus's bicep.

Marcus couldn't help but laugh as Puppy began barking at Gavin. It appeared that he didn't like Daddy number one beating up Daddy number two.

"Traitor," Gavin said, nuzzling his head into Puppy, clearly trying to keep his smile buried in his fur.

It had been about a year since the babbling spitfire came tumbling into Marcus's life. And it was the happiest, most annoying, and greatest year of his life.

Who needs peace and quiet, or covers at all, when you

can spend your days with a man who doesn't stop talking, who insists on sleeping with you as their blanket, and never stops making you smile?

He used to believe that love was a luxury he couldn't afford. That, because of who he was and the responsibilities that came with being the leader of the Shadow Vipers, being in love would only be a distraction. One that could put everybody's lives at risk.

But as it was quickly pointed out to him, his crew were not children. While they might act like them at times, they were fully functioning adults who knew how to take care of themselves and what needed to be done to keep the crew safe and the money rolling in.

It helped, too, that Gavin seemed to understand the family he was stepping into—the chaos, the complications, and the kinds of situations he would inevitably find himself tangled in if he chose to stay in Marcus's life.

And thankfully, Gavin appeared way too obsessed with Marcus's dick to ever think about leaving his sorry ass.

Marcus chuckled at that thought.

"What?" Gavin asked, staring up at him with those gorgeous blue eyes of his.

"Nothing. I just love your stupid ass," Marcus said, leaning in and kissing him on the forehead. Puppy jumped in on the excitement and started licking them both excitedly.

Gavin laughed and reached for his phone.

"Smile!" He laughed as he snapped a photo of the three of them. He opened his social media app and posted the picture for all his followers to see.

While Gavin no longer needed their validation, he once told Marcus that he wanted to continue posting about his life, giving his followers hope that they, too, could find their Prince Charming and a happily ever after one day.

Of course, Gavin heavily edited what he posted online —no crew business or anything illegal. But his followers did know he was dating a handsome biker dude, who rocked his world in more than one way.

When it came to Gavin and coping with the execution of the Valentine Killer, Marcus believed Gavin was doing well. He stopped having nightmares almost immediately after Clive's death and no longer seemed as jittery when left alone in the house.

Marcus offered to take him to therapy, but Gavin just smiled and said his dick was all the therapy he would ever need. So Marcus made sure they attended "therapy" every night and occasionally in the morning when Gavin was feeling a little... *antsy*.

Staring out at the yard full of laughter and family, Marcus still couldn't believe that this was his life.

He had a guy who loved him. A brother who always had his back. And a crew full of people who would step in front of a bullet for him.

This was love.
This was family.
This was his world.

The End

ABOUT THE AUTHOR

Matthew Dante is a Canadian author who writes LGBTQ+ Romances with a rougher twist. He graduated with a Major in Criminology and has been working in the financial crimes industry for over twenty years. He is an avid reader, world traveler, lover of all things Marvel and DC, and a romantic at heart.

As an author, your reviews are very important because they give potential readers a reason to try our books. If you enjoyed reading this book or others, please consider taking a few moments to leave a review.

To stay up to date on all of Matthew Dante's workings, consider joining his newsletter and following him on all his social media platforms. Also, check out his website at matthewdante.com.

ACKNOWLEDGMENTS

I want to take a moment to thank you, my amazing readers. Without your love, support, and enthusiasm, none of these stories would have ever been written. You can't imagine how wonderful it feels to receive a message from a reader who just finished reading your book and tells you they can't wait to read your next one. These simple words have a tremendous effect on us authors. It is this excitement and love that inspires us to work tirelessly to create that perfect story we all hope you will love.

Also, I wanted to thank my wonderful family, who keep me smiling and are always happy to listen to me freak out or complain when I am stuck on a story arc. Your words of encouragement always help me see the brighter side of things.

As for the Bikers of Mayhem? Their story will never be over. Stay tuned!

BOOKS BY MATTHEW DANTE

MM DARK ROMANCE

BIKERS OF MAYHEM:

Primal Urges (Book 1)

Hidden Desires (Book 2)

Carnal Sin (Book 3)

Untamed Aggression (Book 4)

ROUGH EDGES:

Laying Claim (Book 1)

Protecting His (Book 2)

Devouring Sin (Book 3)

Avenging Des (Book 4)

Defending You (Book 5)

Obeying Orders (Book 6)

BOOK OF SIN:

The Collector (Book 1)

The Broker (Book 2)

The Chameleon (Book 3)

The Chemist (Book 4)

FRACTURED SERIES:

Fractured Love (Book 1)

Fractured Mind (Book 2)

Fractured Soul (Book 3)

As I Say...

The Naughty List

MM ROMANCE

Love to Hate You

The Devil Wears Pink

A Campfire Confession (Packing: An MM Anthology)

A Christmas Conundrum (Romance in Winter Anthology)

www.ingramcontent.com/pod-product-compliance
Lightning Source LLC
LaVergne TN
LVHW010640110826
845149LV00014B/2900

9781997751069